Author's Note

I fell in love with Cyrano de Bergerac many years ago. It didn't matter that he was over three hundred years old and I was only nineteen. (His story, told in a play by the same name, is set in 1640.) Cyrano was everything I wanted in a man—a fearless soldier, as full of laughter and poetry and tenderness as he was of fire and passion.

When LOVESWEPT decided to put together a month of **TREASURED TALES**, I knew I had to write Cyrano's story. I gave him a fighter jet instead of a sword, a U.S. Navy uniform rather than a plumed hat, a Kentucky background instead of French. But I kept his fire, his passion, his poetry.

I'm in love with my new Cyrano, Sid Granger, and I hope you'll fall in love with him too.

Writing romance is always a labor of love for me, but it is never easy. I want my characters to come alive for you. I want them to make you laugh and make you cry. But most of all I want them to be unforgettable, so that days or even years later you'll remember them and smile.

And so . . . here is the story of Sid and his beautiful Rose Anne. My gift to you. A gift of love. I hope you will receive this gift as generously as you have in the past. Your loyalty is precious to me.

Thank you for reading my stories, for loving them, and for writing to tell me so.

Peggy Webb

WHAT ARE *LOVESWEPT* ROMANCES?

They are stories of true romance and touching emotion. We believe those two very important ingredients are constants in our highly sensual and very believable stories in the *LOVESWEPT* line. Our goal is to give you, the reader, stories of consistently high quality that may sometimes make you laugh, sometimes make you cry, but are always fresh and creative and contain many delightful surprises within their pages.

Most romance fans read an enormous number of books. Those they truly love, they keep. Others may be traded with friends and soon forgotten. We hope that each *LOVESWEPT* romance will be a treasure—a "keeper." We will always try to publish

LOVE STORIES YOU'LL NEVER FORGET
BY AUTHORS YOU'LL ALWAYS REMEMBER

The Editors

Loveswept ® 593

Peggy Webb
Dark Fire

BANTAM BOOKS

NEW YORK · TORONTO · LONDON · SYDNEY · AUCKLAND

DARK FIRE

A Bantam Book / January 1993

Bantam Books are published by Bantam Books, a division of Bantam Doubleday Dell Publishing Group, Inc. Its trademark, consisting of the words "Bantam Books" and the portrayal of a rooster, is Registered in U.S. Patent and Trademark Office and in other countries. Marca Registrada. Bantam Books, 666 Fifth Avenue, New York, New York 10103.

Acknowledgments

I could not have written this book without the help of several people: friend and fellow writer Laura Taylor and her husband, Gordon, a former Marine Corps F-4 Phantom aviator and TOPGUN graduate, who were endlessly generous and patient in answering all my questions about military service and in providing me with background information about TOPGUN; fellow Tupeloean, Charlie J. Hackett, Sr., aviator and retired U.S. Navy commander; U.S. Navy Recruiting Office, Tupelo; and, of course, my friend and my director in Tupelo Community Theater's production of *The Lion, the Witch, and the Wardrobe,* Tom Wicker, who gave me permission to use his beautiful sonnet. My heartfelt thanks to all of you. I took literary license and changed Tom's autumn to summer, and any mistakes I've made in portraying the men in the U.S. Navy are entirely my own.

"Yes, that is Love—that wind of terrible and jealous beauty, blowing over me—that dark fire, that music . . ."

from *Cyrano de Bergerac*
by EDMOND ROSTAND

One

The roar of jets filled the skies.

Lieutenant Commander Sid Granger felt the familiar surge of adrenaline as the formation of sleek fighters streaked into the blue, their slim noses pointed toward the sun. F-14 Tomcats, looking as fierce as their name, piloted by the navy's finest, the TOPGUNs.

Sid shaded his eyes against the sun, following the formation of jets until there was nothing left to see except a series of contrails snaking white against the hard azure California sky.

"It makes you want to be up there, doesn't it, Eagle?"

"Always." Sid watched the last of the plumed contrails break apart and billow wide until they were a part of the vast blue horizon, then turned to the speaker, a fellow instructor at the U.S. Navy Fighter Weapons School. "But not enough to stick around Miramar and cancel my leave," he added with a grin.

"Thirty days in Paris. Thirty days of French wine and French women." Macky "Hellcat" Waynesboro placed his hand reverently over his heart. "Do the navy proud, Eagle. Kiss them all at least once."

"Me? With this nose that launched a thousand ships? With this face that looks like a hatchet with ears?" Sid laughed. "I'll do well if they don't run screaming at the sight of me and throw themselves into the Seine."

Macky tilted his head and studied his friend, seeing beneath the laughter. Sid Granger had earned the call sign Eagle partly because of his fierceness in the skies and partly because of his looks. He was a big, rawboned man with the noble nose and the fighting spirit of his Kentucky-hills ancestors. A giant in the skies and in the classroom, he was unaccountably distant with most women.

"You underestimate your charms," Macky said lightly. "Wait till you get to Paris. Women are going to fall all over you."

"More than likely, they'll trip over my nose." At Macky's aggrieved look, Sid added, "But I'll kiss at least one, just for you."

"Is that a promise?"

"You can put money on it."

Sid stuffed his hands in the pockets of his flight suit and went off, whistling. It was a good exit, one designed to cover his dismay at the thought of making good his promise.

Sid was the first to arrive in Paris. The others would come later, his buddies, all graduates of the same class at Annapolis, lean, hard men who had been selected during their careers to go to TOP-GUN.

Paris was the chosen rendezvous site because of the air show. Men who loved the skies never got far from them . . . even when they were on leave.

Sid slung his bag over his shoulder and walked

across the cobblestone courtyard. For his thirty-day leave he had taken a second-story apartment in a building known for charm and quaintness rather than glitz and glamour. The rooms were open and airy, with wide French windows that faced the courtyard. The furniture was antique rather than modern, the plumbing adequate rather than admirable, and the staff discreet rather than intrusive.

The Château de l'Ange. House of the Angel, so named because the builder's young fiancée had perished in a fire in the west wing and was said to still walk the halls in search of her lover. The romantic legend appealed to Sid's poetic soul.

When he reached the middle of the courtyard he set down his guitar case and his bag, then breathed deeply of the heavily perfumed air. Roses were everywhere, planted in fat pots sitting at the carved feet of wooden benches, trained into trellises on the brick walls, shaped into trees in enormous stone urns. The courtyard was one of the reasons he kept coming back.

That, and the grand piano that would be waiting for him in his apartment. Here in the House of the Angel his creative spirit always took flight.

"Hello, Paris. I'm back."

A breeze whispered through the rosebushes. Sid smiled. It was enough welcome for him.

The iron gate at the entrance to the courtyard creaked open. Sid turned at the sound and was immediately stricken with a paralysis that constricted his breathing and rooted his feet to the ground. Two women were coming through the gate, one with the red hair and friendly face of a spaniel puppy and the build of a stuffed chair.

It was the other one who took Sid's breath away. She was dressed in white—a soft, filmy skirt that floated around her legs, a diaphanous blouse that bared her shoulders, and a long chiffon scarf that hugged her neck, then floated behind her like a cloud. She was holding on to the older woman's arm, looking down at her and laughing at something one of them had said.

Her face was glorious. It looked as if it had been designed by angels and sculpted with roses. Delicate brows arched over wide-set eyes. A perfect nose balanced above beautifully carved lips. High cheekbones were a perfect counterpoint for a sweetly curving chin. A soft pink blush tinged her creamy skin.

"Oh, look, Rose Anne," the older one said in the distinct drawl of the Deep South.

Her voice spurred Sid to action. He picked up his belongings and ducked behind a grouping of rose trees. Avoidance was always his best tactic with beautiful women. He was spared having to make jokes about his nose, and they were spared having to pretend they didn't notice it. Besides that, the woman called Rose Anne probably wouldn't be caught dead in the company of any man who didn't look like an ad for one of those expensive weekends on the Riviera. He looked more like a coat hanger than a bronzed weekend Romeo.

From the cover of the rose trees he stared at her. She was so beautiful, he felt that looking was almost a sacrilege.

Rose Anne. What a name. Like music.

"They've planted white roses again," the one with the red hair said. "Last time we were here they were all gone. Dead of some terrible scourge or other, I think the gardener told me."

"Aphids, Auntie," the beautiful Rose Anne said, laughing as she hurried across the courtyard. "It was the aphids that killed all the white roses."

White roses? Were they coming his way? Sid quickly surveyed the roses in front of his nose.

Red. He was safe . . . unless they wanted to inspect the red roses too.

Rose Anne bent over the white roses, her white dress and scarf billowing around her. Sid's heart pounded as he watched her. She looked like something sent down from heaven, something pure and untouchable.

The other woman hovered nearby, her eyes darting about like hunting dogs searching for fallen birds.

Sid tried to make himself a part of the scenery. If they spotted him, he would say he was the gardener, looking for aphids. Or maybe the brickmason come to inspect the courtyard's ancient fountain. Or the new cook, hired to bring genuine American cuisine to the patrons.

Anything but what he was. Fighter pilots were supposed to be like Macky "Hellcat" Waynesboro and William "Gunslinger" McGuire and Ron "Hawk" Hiddleston—cool-headed and certain with the women, charming, debonair, and handsome. The only women he'd ever been certain with were his mother, his two sisters, and sweet country girls like Erma June Fortenberry from Hollow Stump, Kentucky, who used to sit beside him on the front porch swing in the summers and talk about her strawberry jam and her pickled peaches.

Sweat inched from under his hair and ran down the sides of his cheeks. He had been cooler facing enemy fire.

"Do you think Antoine will mind if I pick one?" As she turned to face the woman she called "Auntie," the sun struck Rose Anne's eyes. They were a brilliant and riveting green.

"Lord, honey . . . Antoine wouldn't care if you beheaded his entire rose garden. He worships the ground you walk on. He'd die if you stayed at some fancy hotel instead of his place."

"We'll give him something he loves in return." Rose Anne carefully plucked a white rose. "Maybe a box of chocolates. He loves sweets."

"Or another signed photograph of you. I think he's planning to start his own Rose Anne museum."

Rose Anne held the flower to her nose, closing her eyes to inhale the fragrance. "Hmmm, lovely."

In his rose-scented lair, Sid stole secret moments with the forbidden beauty. The nearness of her sang through him with a wild joy that was almost terrifying. Was it love, coming so suddenly through the garden gate? He was an aviator, trained for war. What did he know of romance?

Tucking the flower behind her ear, Rose Anne opened her eyes and stared across the courtyard. For a moment Sid thought he had been found out. He clenched his jaw and waited.

"We're going to be late, Rose Anne."

"I know." Rose Anne sighed. "I wish I could just sit in this garden in the sunshine for the rest of the afternoon."

"And burn your skin? Old Charlie would blow a gasket."

"He would, wouldn't he?" Rose Anne linked her arm through the older woman's and headed for the gate.

Sid waited until the gate closed and the murmur of their voices faded to silence before he left his place among the roses. Taking his belongings, he hurried to the apartment entrance. He took the stairs two at a time, his bag slung over his shoulder and his guitar banging against his legs.

The apartment was cool and inviting. A grand piano gleamed in the sunshine beside the French windows.

Sid stowed his gear in the closet, then crossed to the piano. Leaning down, he ran his hands lightly over the keys, testing their action, their tune.

He was tired from his long flight. Almost exhausted. Taking a nap would be smart. Then he would be fresh and ready to go when his buddies arrived.

As he started from the piano, a vision of Rose Anne's face rose before him. He sank onto the piano bench once more, filled with a dark fire, a music of jealous and terrible beauty that swept through his soul.

His hands began to move over the keyboard.

"Here she is! Everybody, here she is!" Charlie Lazarre, Rose Anne's manager, trotted toward her like a Shetland pony, his squat legs racing to outdistance his pot belly. Red in the face from his efforts, he arrived puffing and wiping the sweat on his face with a polka dot linen handkerchief.

Cooing like a pouter pigeon, he bent over her hand. "You look ravishing, my dear. Ravishing." Straightening up, he anxiously patted a curl on her cheek blown loose by the wind. "The Paris press is going to love you. They already love you."

"Quit hovering, Charlie. That's my job." Bitsy Rucker planted herself squarely between Charlie and her niece. "Why don't we go over there and dig into that pile of fattening goodies and leave our girl to do what she does best . . . charm the press. Besides that, you're going to work yourself up into a heart attack one of these days."

"You're right, Bitsy. She'll charm them. Charm them." Charlie went toward the dessert table, still wiping the perspiration.

Bitsy leaned to whisper in Rose Anne's ear, "I'm going to sneak you some chocolate-covered strawberries when Charlie's not looking."

Chocolate was forbidden on Rose Anne's austere diet, as were whipped cream and butter and nuts and every other delicacy that would put an ounce of fat on her willowly body.

"Just one," she said.

"The saint's drawers! If I had your discipline, I'd a been president of the United States by now instead of an old biddy following you around the globe." Bitsy cast a practiced eye in the direction of the press hounds waiting for the kill. "Watch that slick-looking number with the twirly mustache. He reminds me of the one in Rome who tried to sneak into your bedroom dressed as a florist's delivery boy. If he gives you any trouble, just holler and I'll come running with a big stick."

"You worry too much, Auntie." Rose Anne patted her hand. "Go and enjoy the food."

"I will. Especially since I'm eating for two." She always took an extra helping in the name of her niece, who was, in her opinion, being starved to death for no good reason.

Bitsy left to join Charlie, muttering under her breath about the world's obsession with "skin and bones." Smiling, Rose Anne turned to meet the paparazzi.

Darkness curtained the courtyard. The white roses she had admired earlier were now mere shadows in the black-velvet night that had fallen over Paris.

Rose Anne stood on her balcony, delicately munching the forbidden chocolate strawberry and enjoying the cool breeze that whispered over her skin. The heady perfume of roses wafted upward from below.

Somewhere in the heart of Paris, lovers would be holding each other in candlelit nightclubs, dancing with their cheeks pressed close and their bodies touching. Sighing, she closed her mouth around the rich, juicy berry.

She envied them, those careless lovers free to flirt and dance until two and gorge themselves without worrying about dark circles under their eyes or extra pounds on their hips or even worse— unscrupulous people who might be using them for their own selfish purposes. To be free. To be loved for herself rather than her fame and her face.

In the beginning of her career it hadn't mattered. She had chosen her path, and she was happy. But lately she found herself filled with a strange nostalgia, as if she had left something precious behind in the marshy depths of south Georgia, as if there were secret wonders that had gone undiscovered when she'd taken the path to fame.

"I'm going to watch television, Rose Anne. Want to join me?" Bitsy, wearing a pink silk nightcap over her flaming red curls, joined Rose Anne on the balcony.

"What is it?"

"An old Grace Kelly movie. She was nearly as beautiful as you are." Bitsy leaned over the railing and inhaled the night air. "Smells like home."

"Are you homesick, Auntie?"

"Heck, no. You know me. Give me a good sturdy pair of shoes and a plane ticket, and I'll go anywhere . . . including, by George, Africa."

Rose Anne had forgotten about Africa. Three years earlier the thought of going on location there filled her with anticipation. Now it filled her with dread. The heat. The flies. The incessant hum of insects.

She sat on the railing and gazed out over the courtyard, the half-eaten strawberry clutched in her hand, forgotten. From across the way came the strains of music.

"Do you hear that, Auntie?"

Bitsy cocked her head toward the sound.

"Sounds like they're trying to rip the ivories off the piano."

"It's beautiful."

"Beautiful . . . but sad." The breeze threatened to rob Bitsy of her nightcap. She ducked back inside. "Lord, I can't listen to that anymore. If I do, I'm liable to break down and cry." She patted Rose Anne's arm. "You stay if you want to, but I'm fixing to get settled in with Cary Grant."

"I thought it was Grace Kelly."

"It is, but she's secondary." Bitsy adjusted her cap. "If you had been a movie star instead of a model, I guess we'd be traipsing all over the country with somebody like Cary Grant instead of Charlie."

"You can't fool me. You love Charlie."

"I do, but don't tell him. I don't want him to get a big head."

Bitsy went off to her favorite chair in front of the television set, and Rose Anne went to the open French doors and leaned her head against the door frame. The music wrapped itself around her and she drew it close, feeling it caress her skin, invade her heart.

There was a thunderous crashing chord, and the music ceased. Rose Anne felt deprived, as if someone had suddenly snatched her cloak away and left her shivering in the dark.

"Don't stop," she whispered.

Almost as if he had heard, the musician started playing again. Soon he lifted his voice, rich and deep and mellow. It was music like none she had ever heard, music of such dark and haunting beauty, she felt as if she were touching the man's soul.

Breathless, she pressed her hand to her throat. Instrument and voice blended as one, sending the music across the courtyard like arrows to pierce her heart. The deep fragrance of roses drifted upward and the night brightness of stars shone down as Rose Anne stood in the doorway, invaded by music.

It seemed to be coming from the apartment directly across from hers, but when she looked she could see no lights. Somehow that was appropriate, that the beautiful brooding music should be coming from a dark and mysterious room.

The magnificent voice touched her in ways she had never been touched. She pressed a hand against her throat, feeling the passionate fluttering of her pulse and the increased heat of her skin. The heat flamed through her, ignited by the music and trapped by her clothes. Slowly, she unbuttoned her filmy robe and let it drop to the floor.

A breeze caressed her bare shoulders, but it did nothing to alleviate the flames that still licked her. She was liquid with music and heat and passion.

The music soared around her and over her and through her. She closed her eyes and embraced it.

Without warning, the music stopped. Rose Anne leaned against the door frame with her eyes closed, imprisoned by the intensity of the melody that still echoed through her.

Who was the musician? The creator? Surely it had to be a man of passion and spirit, for how could he be anything less when her heart was stripped bare and her soul was crying out for the dark fire that only he could provide.

She stayed in the open doorway, trapped by secret longings while the full moon shed its splendor in the skies and the roses lent their perfume to the night. She felt a dampness on her cheeks. Slowly she lifted her hands to her face and touched tears.

Across the courtyard in his darkened apartment, Sid stood at his window, watching. The piano was silent now, the music stilled. He had poured out his soul to her, and now she stood in her doorway with the moonlight caressing her skin. Rose Anne. A beautiful, unattainable goddess he only dared dream about.

Except in his music. He had made love to her at the piano, then taken her in his arms and smothered her perfect face with kisses.

Had she heard? Did she know?

Of course not. And she would never know. Nor would the rest of the world. His music was a private pleasure for him, too pure and honest to be corrupted by others.

"You ought to do something with that talent," his best buddy Luther "Lightning" Snell was always telling him. "I bet if the right people heard you sing and play that stuff you write, you'd be so rich, you could buy the navy instead of flying for it."

"My music is private, Luther," he would always say.

And so it was. Selling his music would be like selling his soul.

Sid strained his eyes in the darkness, seeking the lone figure in the French doors across the way. She tilted back her head and stretched her arms out into the night. Her white gown swirled around her legs, caressed her hips, molded itself to her breasts. Moonlight kissed her skin with soft, silvery lips.

No footsteps on the stone courtyard marred the silence, no lights save hers marred the darkness. He was alone with her, alone with the night and his passion.

Two

All the fighter pilots were gathered in a dim, smoky nightclub on the Left Bank—Sid "Eagle" Granger, Ron "Hawk" Hiddleston, William "Gunslinger" McGuire, Luther "Lightning" Snell, Grayson "Panther" Malone. Buddies who had gone through Annapolis together, who had earned their wings together, who had flown the skies when they were friendly and flown when they were full of the enemy, who loved one another and protected one another . . . and who were willing at a moment's notice to die for one another. They were TOPGUNs, the flying elite.

It was the second night of Sid's arrival, the first for his friends. They were high with anticipation and camaraderie and fatigue.

"Hell, Eagle. Don't sit there and tell me you haven't already got a woman stashed away somewhere." Gunslinger McGuire tilted back in his chair, a lean, tall man who still had to look up to be eye to eye with Sid Granger.

"Nope. I've been sightseeing."

"Yeah. Thirty-six, twenty-four, thirty-six . . . thirty-nine, twenty-three, forty." Panther Malone

13

winked across the top of his beer glass at the pretty waitress passing by.

"Forty!" Lightning Snell snorted into his beer. "That's getting a little on the heavy side."

"I like my women with plenty of padding." They all laughed, and Panther quaffed his beer. Suddenly he set the glass on the table with a thunk. "Wait a minute! Hold everything! Look at what just walked through the door."

Sid almost lost his breath. Rose Anne was poised in the doorway, a red dress of soft cloudlike material floating around her. She wore no jewelry, for the only adornment she needed was her perfect face.

At her side was the woman she called Auntie, glowering around the room as if she expected to fend off attackers at any minute.

"Good Lord." Gunslinger McGuire lifted his beer reverently to his heart.

"I couldn't have said it better myself." Panther never took his eyes off Rose Anne as she glided across the room. Nor did the rest of them. "She's the most beautiful thing I've ever seen.

"Fellows," he added, turning around to grin at them. "I've just changed my mind about padded women."

"Who is she?" Luther Snell asked, propping his elbows on the table and gazing at her like a lovestruck teenager.

She was four tables away, out of hearing range but not out of view. The music of her soared through Sid's soul. *Who is she?* he thought. *She's a vision, a dream.*

"Her name is Rose Anne, and her picture is on the cover of every magazine from here to eternity." Everybody turned to stare at Hawk Hiddleston. He gave them his famous grin. "She's known in the modeling world as the Face, and that formidable lady with her is Bitsy Rucker, aptly called the Dragon because she never lets a man within fifteen feet of her famous niece."

"How did you know all that?" Gunslinger asked.

"Inside information." Hawk winked.

"His wife," Luther added.

Hawk was the only one of them who was married. Panther and Gunslinger had had wives, two apiece, but couldn't seem to get one with staying power. Lightning and Eagle had never come close to the altar.

"Don't tell her we saw the Face," Hawk said. "If you do, she'll wonder why I didn't come back with an autograph."

The five pilots gazed across the room at the Face, each with his separate fantasy.

"I've got more in mind than an autograph," Gunslinger said.

"Yeah. Lots more. In fact . . ." Grinning, Panther reached into his pocket and pulled out a bill. "Here's fifty that says I can win her attentions before any of you dogs."

"You're on." Gunslinger plunked down his fifty.

"I don't know . . ." Lightning said. Although he had the disposition of a saint and the face of an angel, he was almost tongue-tied around women. It came from growing up with six sisters who never let him get a word in edgewise.

"Well, I do. If I enter the fray, all of you would lose." Hawk lifted his beer, leaned back in his chair, and grinned. "Of course, I'd have to learn to live without that part of my anatomy I prize so highly. My wife's already given me fair warning."

Amid the laughter, Sid watched Rose Anne. She looked out of place in a dimly lit club, too pure, too beautiful for the smoky, slightly sleazy atmosphere. She sat in her chair, tall and regal, taking everything in with her eyes incredibly bright and impossibly green. A half smile played around her lips.

She was worth more than a fifty-dollar bet.

He turned back to his buddies and pinned Panther down with his dark, piercing eyes. "I want to know what you mean by 'winning her attentions.'"

"Hell, Eagle. You know I wouldn't propose anything illegal and ignoble with you around. I don't want to get my Iowa butt whipped with your Kentucky principles." Panther leaned across the table to Sid. "How about, whoever gets her on the dance floor first?"

Sid glanced at Rose Anne, then back to Panther. "I can live with that."

"Are you in?" Panther asked him.

"No. I've got two left feet. My nose keeps me off balance."

"Count me out too." Luther Snell pretended a great interest in his beer. "You know how my tongue gets tangled. I'd probably call her a 'braving rudy' or something equally as foolish."

"Dancing's too easy anyhow. You know she's going to dance with the first one of us who gets to the table. Who could turn any of us down?" Panther reached for a handful of pretzels, then considered as he chewed. "How about this . . . the dancing is just a prelude. Whoever gets her out to dinner first wins the pot."

"I'll drink to that." Gunslinger lifted his glass. "Lightning? Eagle?"

"Count me out." Sid was not about to pursue that impossible dream, and certainly not for a wager.

"I'll still have to pass." Lightning glanced at Rose Anne and sighed. "Lord, what a shame. If I had the gift of words, I'd tell her . . . hey, wait a minute." He turned on Sid. "Eagle?"

"No." Sid held up one hand. "Forget it."

"Aw, come on, Eagle. You know I get damned near tongue-tied with women, and I'm already half in love with her." Lightning added the clencher. "Be my mouthpiece. Just this once. Just until she agrees to dinner."

Sid gazed across the room at Rose Anne. She was beyond his reach. There was no question about it. But Luther, with his angelic face, had a chance.

How he would love to court her. He would use poetry straight from the heart and music ripped out of his soul. Speaking for Luther, he could say all the things to her that he'd never dare say if he were speaking for himself.

A vision of her in the courtyard bending over the white rose came to him. Suddenly, the idea of wooing her anonymously took on a kind of appeal.

"I'll do it," he said before he changed his mind. "I'll be your spokesman, Lightning. Hand me that napkin."

Sid pulled out his pen and began to write.

"One of them is coming your way, Rose Anne."

"Which one, Auntie?"

"The tall, rawboned one."

Rose Anne didn't look, but merely folded her hands in her lap, waiting. She'd seen the table full of men when she came in. They were hard to miss, men filled with a vitality and a sense of daring that was almost palpable.

Bitsy patted her hand. "Don't worry, dear. I'll make quick work of him."

"No." Rose Anne's reply startled them both. She settled back in her chair and tried to think why she would want to have anything to say to a man who didn't know her, a man who probably had recognized her and was obviously on the make.

It was something about his eyes, she guessed. They were dark and haunting, even across the room. She hadn't meant to stare, but she couldn't keep herself from looking.

"It's all right, Auntie. I didn't come here tonight to get picked up, and I'm not about to let that happen. But I don't mind if all he wants to do is talk."

"You're lonesome, aren't you, honey?"

"Maybe. Just a little bit. I think it's because of that music I heard last night." She hadn't wanted to come to the nightclub, not really. But something about that music had made her restless. This brief outing was her way of holding the blues at bay . . . if only for a little while.

The tall man bore down on them, merely a table away. Curious now, Rose Anne studied him out of the corner of her eye. He was almost noble-looking, but certainly not handsome.

"This one looks harmless enough," Bitsy said. "I'll go powder my nose, but if he gives you any trouble, just give a holler and I'll . . ."

". . . come running with a big stick." Rose Anne waved Bitsy off, laughing.

She felt his presence before he spoke. He was a large shadow, towering over her. She felt the heat of him, the power of him.

"Hello," he said politely. "My name is Sid Granger. I'm in Paris on leave with some of my navy buddies."

Military, Rose Anne thought. She might have guessed. That accounted for the sense of danger that hovered over him.

She smiled at him. Up close, his eyes were almost frightening in their intensity. She pressed one hand to the pulse fluttering in her throat.

"Do you mind if I sit down?"

His voice. Why did it make her think of that dark night music?

"Not at all," she managed to say.

He didn't sit in the chair next to hers and try to

press his legs against her thighs as so many before him had. Instead, he took the chair across the table in a gesture of old-fashioned courtliness. Maybe she was mistaken about him. Maybe he was different from all the others.

"You are Rose Anne, I believe."

"Yes." So he did know. Somehow that disappointed her. "Jones," she added.

"I'm very pleased to meet you, Miss Jones."

Miss Jones? She felt almost as if she had stepped back into the nineteenth century.

"I hear the cadences of the South in your voice, Mr. Granger."

"Just Sid . . . I'm from a long line of Grangers who have never gotten far from the Kentucky border. Most of them believe Paris is on another planet."

"Sometimes I think that too."

Rose Anne relaxed. This man was easy to talk to in spite of that deep, dark voice that sent shivers along her spine.

"Are you here for business or pleasure?"

"A modeling assignment. Strictly business." She smiled at him. "I stole this evening for pleasure . . . though I can't stay long."

"In that case, you should take advantage of every moment. Do you enjoy dancing?"

"I haven't danced in so long." Was he asking her?

"Then you should."

They watched each other across the table, and she waited. *One dance,* she thought. She would allow herself one dance, and then she would go home, back to that quiet apartment with nobody to disturb her sleep, nobody to take her in his arms and keep her awake with his passion, nobody to intrude upon the hours she needed for beauty sleep.

She was very close to wallowing in self-pity.

Angry at herself, she jerked her attention back to the moment and the man across the table from her. He seemed to be considering far more than one dance.

"I have a friend," he finally said.

"A friend?"

"Lieutenant Luther Snell. He's a great pilot and a very fine gentleman." Sid Granger propped his elbows on the table and leaned toward her, his face intense.

"The only problem with Luther is that he's extremely shy with women, and he's asked me to be his mouthpiece."

"Is this some kind of joke, Mr. Granger?"

"Sid." He fixed his long hands into a careful steeple, then gazed at her over the tips of his fingers. "I know this must sound strange to you—"

"That's an understatement."

"Unbelievable?" He grinned at her.

It was such a lopsided, friendly grin, she couldn't resist smiling back.

"You're getting close," she said.

"Would you settle for weird?"

"Yes. Now, if you will excuse me, I think I see my aunt coming." She made a move to stand.

"Please don't go. Not yet." He reached across the table and touched her hand. Rose Anne didn't expect the sharp awareness that jolted through her.

Sid withdrew his hand and pulled a folded paper napkin from his pocket. "Luther is shy in person but not on paper." He handed the napkin to her. "Would you please read this before you go?"

Intrigued, Rose Anne unfolded the napkin. The words were written in bold strokes with black ink. It didn't look like the work of a shy man.

"Your beauty is as rare as the white rose," the note read, "and just as sweet. One dance, fair lady, I beg of you. And I will treat you as gently as the most delicate flower in the courtyard."

Rose Anne sucked in her breath. The white rose? The courtyard? Could it be that this Luther Snell, this man too shy to ask for a dance in person, was the same man who made beautiful music in the dark?

She carefully refolded the napkin. "Where is he?"

Triumph and jealousy warred in Sid. Triumph won. Luther was his best friend. He deserved a woman like Rose Anne.

"Over there." He nodded toward his table. Hawk and Gunslinger and Panther and Lightning were all craning their necks, trying to make out what was going on between him and the Face. "The one with curly blond hair and the face like a movie star."

"And he wrote this?" Rose Anne tapped a slender finger with a delicate pink nail against the note.

"He sent it to you." Skirting the truth made Sid feel like a heel. Honesty was a point of honor with him. And yet, how could he quibble over one small lie when he had agreed to the biggest lie of all . . . courting a woman under the guise of friendship.

After tonight he was finished with this game. He would get them to call off the whole damned thing. And if they refused, he would pay Luther's fifty and let the rest of them do what they wanted. His conscience would be clear.

"Tell him yes."

"Yes?" Sid had almost hoped she would say no. Then the whole thing would be over.

"Are you so surprised? Not only is the note poetic, but if the man is as fine as you say he is, I'd be a fool to turn him down." She smiled. "You've done your job well, Sid Granger. Go tell your friend I'll give him one dance."

Sid slid back his chair. "He will be honored." He left the table quickly, without looking back.

"Hey, Eagle. What's the news?" Luther asked.

Sid dragged back his chair, straddled it, then took a long drink of beer.

"The way he's glowering, the news has to be bad. Right, Eagle?" Panther pounded him on the back. "Now, boys, watch how a real man does it."

"Wrong, Panther." Sid set his glass down with such force he jarred the table. "The lady said yes."

"She said yes?" Luther's elation lasted only seconds, then he tightened his jaw. "Now what am I going to do?"

Sid pinned Luther down with fierce eyes. "Don't get fresh with her. Don't hold her too close, and none of that rubbing your hands all over her back. She's not a prize; she's a lovely and sensitive woman."

"Hell, Eagle. You sound like her mother." Panther gave Eagle a wicked, knowing grin. He had always been able to see through deception.

Sid moderated his approach. He had no desire for Panther or anybody else to discover his motives. "Just say I'm keeping my nose to the ground, sniffing out trouble before it starts." He grinned at them, then turned to Luther. "Get on over there before the lady changes her mind."

"Yes sir." Luther snapped a salute, straightened his tie, then marched stiffly across the room.

"Hell, if he doesn't loosen up, he'll break before he even gets her in his arms." Gunslinger scooted back his chair to get a better view of Rose Anne's table.

The rest of the pilots followed suit. Everybody except Sid. He had no intention of giving himself away by such blatant behavior.

Across the room Luther bent over Rose Anne.

She took his hand and allowed him to lead her onto the small, crowded dance floor.

Sid doubled his hands into fists and clenched his jaw. Luther would have to hold her close. There was no preventing it.

The band was playing a slow and easy blues song, just right for cuddling cheek to cheek and dancing hip to hip. Sid thanked God he was tall enough so that he didn't have to crane his neck to see. Luther's arms were around Rose Anne, his chest pressed close enough to graze her breasts.

A muscle ticked in the side of Sid's jaw. He would break Lightning into small pieces if he took advantage of her on the dance floor.

The music pounded through his head. Luther moved stiffly on the floor, but Rose Anne floated, her dress flowing about her like a gentle red wind. Her skin was exquisite under the lights, petal soft and glowing. Her hands looked like flowers nestled in Luther's big paws.

"Look at old Lightning go." Gunslinger reached over and clapped Sid on the shoulder. "You should be proud of your handiwork, Eagle. It looks like a romance in the making."

Sid couldn't reply. He was on the dance floor heart and mind and soul. Every beat of the music pulsed through his body. He felt the movement of Rose Anne's body, savored the silkiness of her skin, heard the soft rise and fall of her breathing.

The sounds of his friends' voices swirled around him, but he didn't hear what they were saying. His entire focus was on the dance floor. His heart and mind were filled with the vision in red.

When the song came to an end, Luther escorted Rose Anne back to her table, guiding her through the crowded club with a hand on her elbow. Sid didn't breathe easily until Luther left her with the Dragon and headed back to the table.

"Way to go, Lightning." Panther pounded him

on the back. "But the bet's not won. You still have to get her out to dinner."

"The bet's off," Sid said.

They all looked at him as if he had suddenly grown stripes and turned into a zebra.

"What do you mean, the bet's off?" Panther, always the most vocal, was the first to speak.

"Just what I said. She's not some prize at a county fair that goes to the highest bidder. She's a person."

"She's a whole hell of a lot more than that." Panther spoke with reverent passion. "She's a sports car among pickup trucks. What's the harm in a little wager over dinner?"

Hawk and Gunslinger chimed in, siding with Panther. The good-natured argument raged around Luther, who sat drinking his beer and watching the woman in red.

"Sid's right," he finally said. "Anyhow, every-thing has changed."

"What do you mean?" Sid turned to him.

"I don't care about the money anymore." Luther set his beer on the table and faced them all. "I forfeit. I pull out."

"Why?" Panther asked.

"I really like her. I think I'm falling in love."

Sid's heart nosedived. He felt as if he had just bailed out of his plane without a parachute.

"You're in love with her?"

"Not exactly. I don't think it happens that fast."

Yes, it can, Sid thought. *In an instant, true love can walk through a garden gate.*

"What I mean is—" Pausing, Luther ran his hands through his curly hair. "I want to see her again, but not for any bet."

"Well, I'll be damned." Panther sat back in his chair, grinning. "Old Lightning has finally fallen for a woman."

"It's about time." Gunslinger whacked him on

the back. "Go for it, buddy. I did . . . twice. And it was good both times."

Amid the general laughter, Sid glanced across the room. Rose Anne was still at her table, her head bent close to the Dragon.

Was she in love too? It figured. She was beautiful, Luther was handsome. She was gentle, he was kind. They would make a great couple.

He took one last, lingering look at Rose Anne. Letting go of a dream was heart-wrenching, even if the dream was impossible, had been impossible from the very first.

"We're all pulling for you," Sid told Luther. "We'll stand up for you at the wedding."

"I haven't even gotten her to agree to dinner yet."

"She will. Just give her time. Who can resist you?"

"She can. All she talked about was that note you wrote, how poetic it was, how beautiful."

Sid didn't know whether to laugh or to cry. Pride wasn't worth all that much when it was paired with hopelessness.

"I need you, Eagle. I need you to be my mouthpiece."

Panther snorted. "Hell, Lightning. Next thing I know you'll be asking him to do the honors on your wedding night."

"Panther's right. You don't need me. When she gets to know you, she'll love you for yourself. Any woman in her right mind would."

"I can't do it without you, Eagle."

"No."

"As a favor to me . . ."

"I'm sorry. Not this time. Besides, it wouldn't work."

Across the way Rose Anne and her aunt prepared to leave. Even with the distance that separated them, Sid was aware of her slightest movement. His head came up.

She glanced his way and their gazes met and held. He didn't breathe. She didn't move. If the others noticed, they gave no indication.

Heat collected under his collar and sweat rolled down the side of his neck. Sid couldn't have done anything except gaze at her if the club had suddenly caught fire.

She nodded ever so slightly, and her lips curved in that marvelous half smile. The beauty of it dazzled Sid. Even when she turned to go, he sat in his chair, paralyzed.

"Sid . . ."

Rose Anne was at the door. He watched until there was nothing left to see, not even a glimpse of red.

"What?" He turned slowly, like a man coming out of a trance.

"I said I'm calling in a favor." Luther looked him straight in the eye. "For saving your butt over the Gulf."

Filled with Rose Anne, with his vision of her, his dreams of her, Sid slowly nodded.

"Does that mean yes? You'll give me the right words to court her?"

At that moment Sid would have sold his soul to the devil merely for the right to gaze at her from behind prison bars.

"I'll do it, Luther. I'll win the fair Rose Anne for you."

Three

Sid left the club early, excusing himself by telling his buddies he had to prepare a courtship plan for Luther. *Lies. All lies.*

Two days in Paris, and he had changed from an honorable, loyal man to one full of deception and dark secrets. He was going to prepare a courtship plan all right, but it would be *his* heart he was pouring out to Rose Anne, his case he was stating. And all the while hiding behind Luther's handsome face.

The bitter irony was that his plan was already working. He was winning her for another man.

When he reached his apartment, he poured out his passion at the piano.

Across the courtyard Rose Anne lay in her bed, flat on her back so she wouldn't get pillow creases in her face as she slept. Soft night winds billowed the curtains at her open windows, bringing in the perfume of the rose garden. And with the wind came the music.

When the first notes sounded, Rose Anne clutched her sheet and brought it up around her chin. The music was frighteningly passionate and darkly sensual. It invaded her.

She clung to the sheet as if it would protect her from the fierce, seductive music. Her skin tingled. Her body heat increased. Restless, she tossed in the bed. The sheet dragged and pulled at her body like hot hands while the wild music swirled through her.

Her breasts felt heavy, turgid, their nipples peaked and straining at the thin fabric of her gown. She cupped them, lifting them as if they were an offering to the dark god of music.

The frantic musical rhythm pulsed through her. Groaning, she moved to its beat. The sheet tangled around her, touching her, holding her, seducing her.

Rose Anne bit her bottom lip hard. And still the music invaded her. Enslaved by a nameless hunger, she welcomed it, embraced it. The music was demon lover, filling her with liquid fire.

On and on the music played. Shining beads of sweat rolled between her breasts, slicked her thighs. The music pounded at her without mercy.

"Please," she begged. "Please." She didn't know whether she was begging it to stop or begging for more.

The music swelled and throbbed. Rose Anne trembled at its majesty, its power. Relentless, it washed over her, and she rode the waves. Higher and higher it carried her, its chords vibrating through her with dark intensity.

When she thought she could endure no more, when she thought she might shatter into a million bright pieces, the music came to a thundering, crashing climax. Slack, Rose Anne sagged against the sheets.

Echoes of music pulsed through the room, charging the silence with electricity. Rose Anne lay unmoving until the last echo died away, and then she reached to her night stand. Her hand touched the note. In the dark she clutched it to her breast.

"Luther," she whispered.

On the other side of the courtyard Sid pressed his hot forehead against the cool polished wood on the piano.

"Rose Anne," he whispered.

The day's shoot was in the Luxembourg Gardens. Rose Anne sat in the trailer that served as her portable dressing room while two men worked on her face and one worked on her hair. Charlie hovered nearby, wringing his hands.

"Oh, my dear. Those dark circles under your eyes. And your lip." He patted his face with a yellow striped silk handkerchief. "What happened to your lip?"

Before Rose Anne could explain, Bitsy intervened.

"Now, Charlie, just calm yourself down." She took his elbow and dragged him outside, away from her niece. "No call to upset her. Haven't you ever had a sleepless night?"

"Yes, but she's a model."

"She's human." Bitsy propped her elbows on her hips and glowered at him. "I've seen other models come in looking like death on wheels, and after their makeup is finished they look like a million dollars."

"She's not other models. She's the Face." He swabbed his brow. "What happened anyhow?"

"When I saw her lip this morning, I asked the same thing. All she told me was that she had been restless last night."

"Did she go out?"

"We were at a nightclub for a couple of hours, but I was with her the whole time. She danced one dance, then we came home."

"She didn't go anywhere after that?"

"I'm positive. Besides, Rose Anne is not the sneaky type. She would never go anywhere without telling me, especially considering the disappointments she's had with men."

"All that happened years ago. I though it was behind her."

"If one man breaks your heart, that's not so bad. But when two in a row turn out to be scoundrels, that's harder to get over."

One of the technicians approached Bitsy and Charlie.

"I have a message for Rose Anne." He held out a sheet of paper, folded twice, and a single white rose.

"For Rose Anne?" Bitsy took the paper and the flower. "Who sent it?"

"That gentleman by the tree."

Bitsy looked in the direction he had indicated, and saw the tall sailor from the night before leaning against the tree. When he saw her looking he nodded politely.

"Who is he?" Charlie asked.

"One of the navy pilots from the club last night."

"Good grief. Navy! Throw that note away."

"That's for Rose Anne to decide." Bitsy went inside the trailer.

The makeup and hair people were finished with Rose Anne. Her long, flowing blond hair spilled over her shoulders, her exquisite face was glowing, and her slender body was draped with a forties-style chiffon gown that matched her sea-green eyes. A first glimpse of her would take most people's breath away, but Bitsy was accustomed to having a niece who was considered the most beautiful woman in the world. She didn't even blink an eye.

"I've got a message for you."

Rose Anne's eyes lit up when she saw the white rose. "What's Antoine doing sending me a white rose?"

"Number one, he didn't send it. Number two, his wife would kill him if he did, even though his feelings are strictly paternal."

"Then who?"

"Read the note and find out."

Rose Anne inhaled the fragrance of the rose, then pressed the soft petals against her cheek. Still holding the rose, she opened the note and began to read.

"Time is but a powerful stead that speeds me to your side. Give me one precious moment of your time, beautiful one, and I will count the day not wasted."

The note was unsigned. Smiling, she folded it carefully and tucked it inside her purse.

"Where is he?" she asked.

"Outside. On the fringes of all this madness Charlie calls a shoot." Rose Anne stood up. "You're going to him?"

"Tell them I'll be back in five minutes." Seeing Bitsy's skeptical look, Rose Anne patted her hand. "I *must* see him, Auntie."

"I'm getting too old for this job of Dragon." Bitsy heaved a resigned sigh. "Be careful, honey."

Rose Anne laughed. "There are at least fifty people milling around here. I'll be as safe as if I were in a church."

Sid's heart leapt when he saw her coming. Two days earlier he might have scoffed at such a romantic notion, but now he accepted it as a fact.

Leaning against the tree, he watched her approach. A breeze swirled her gown around her ankles and molded it to her body. She smiled when she saw him, and lifted her hand in greeting.

His love note had brought her to him. Joy rushed through him, and, on its heels, desire. She was exquisite, sensational, sensuous. He clenched his jaw against the passion and rammed his fists into his pockets to still the joy.

He was there as Luther's representative.

"Hi," she said, stopping so close that her gossamer gown brushed against his legs.

For a moment he was spellbound. The gown was little more than an illusion. Lush rosy nipples pushed against the thin fabric. Creamy skin, shining as if it had been slicked with dew, showed through the slashed opening of her bodice. Her here-to-eternity legs were clearly defined by the thin, billowing gown. The only concession to modesty was a tiny wisp of satin that hugged her hips.

Blood roared in his ears. Passion surged through him. Excitement squeezed his heart. It was the same glorious feeling that came the first moment he lifted a powerful jet toward the endless horizon— the same and yet more, ever so much more.

"How did you find me?" she asked.

"It was easy. Half of Paris is keeping up with the activities of the world's most beautiful model."

"I live in a fishbowl."

"Does it bother you?"

"In the beginning it didn't, but lately . . ." Her sigh was as gentle as the breeze that played in the leaves above their heads. "Sometimes I wish I could spend a day of complete anonymity."

"The Paris Air Show might provide you that escape."

"I've heard of it. Will the crowds be big?"

"So big you would be swallowed up."

"Like Jonah in the whale?"

They laughed together. Instinctively he reached for her hand. It felt like a soft, exotic baby bird resting in his big paws.

"Exactly," he said. "Except that you won't have to wait three days to come back out into the daylight . . . unless you want to."

Her eyes widened and her free hand flew to her throat. Captivated, Sid gazed into her eyes, forgetting that he was courting for Luther.

"Come with me." His voice was deep, urgent, seductive.

Rose Anne met his gaze. His eyes were dark and powerful, fierce and penetrating. Suddenly all the love words on the notes and all the passionate music of the night seemed centered in Sid Granger's eyes. She leaned forward, inexplicably drawn to him. Shivers crawled along her skin, and desire clawed at her loins. She felt her nipples harden.

What was happening? How could this craggy-faced, rugged-looking man cause such sensations? It was the music that seduced her, the crashing, thundering dark music . . . and the notes, the poetic notes written with a bold hand.

They had not come from this man. He was merely Luther's emissary.

"Did Luther send you?" she whispered, and the spell was broken.

Sid released her hand and stepped back, out of the reach of her seductive gown. But even with the small distance he put between them, he could still feel the brush of silk against his legs, still see the tight rosy nipples that strained against her gown, still almost taste the moisture that shimmered on her skin.

"I came for Luther," he said.

"And that beautiful note?"

"I brought it for him."

"Then you're here to invite me to the air show on his behalf?"

"Yes. That was a slip of the tongue earlier. But I *will* be there."

"You'll be there?" Somehow the news quickened her pulse.

"Yes. One of the reasons for spending my leave in Paris is the air show."

"Will I see you?"

Do you want to see me? he longed to ask. But this was Luther's courtship.

A muscle ticked in his tight jaw, and he rammed his fists hard into his pockets.

"You'll see all of us . . . Hawk, Gunslinger, Panther, Lightning."

"Your flying buddies?"

"Yes. Those are our call signs, the names we use to communicate with each other when we're in the air."

"And what is yours?"

"Eagle."

Smiling, she tilted her head to study him. "It's appropriate, I think."

"How?" he asked, forgetting for the moment his eagle's beak that passed for a nose.

"The eagle is a fierce and noble creature, not a beautiful bird, but awesome in its majesty."

He almost grew wings and soared. Reminding himself that women were given to flights of fancy, he kept his feet firmly on the ground.

"Thank you, beautiful lady." He bent gallantly over her hand and pressed his lips to her soft skin. He would remember the taste of her forever. "I don't think that's what my buddies had in mind," he added, laughing.

He didn't know which one of them drew back, but suddenly the contact was broken.

"I have to get back."

She sounded sorry to go. Was she?

"I . . . Luther will pick you up on Saturday. Is ten too early?"

"It's fine. Do you have something to write my address on?"

"I already know it." *It's engraved on my heart.*

She smiled. "Another bit of detective work?"

"Just plain luck. We're staying at the same inn."

Rose Anne grew very still. *The music.* She had known it had come from him. Gazing into his dark eyes, she shivered. *No. Not him.*

"Is Luther staying there too?"

"Yes."

She breathed a sigh of relief. It was Luther who wrote the poetic notes, Luther who composed the hauntingly seductive music.

"Rose Anne!" The sound of Charlie's voice brought her out of the trancelike state she was in. Charlie hurried up, puffing. "They're ready for you, my dear."

She looked into Sid's dark eyes. There was nothing left to say, not even good-bye. She inclined her head as if to seal the bargain, then linked her hand through Charlie's arm and returned to the set.

The photographer, the director, and the technicians were there waiting for her.

"You look stunning, Rose Anne. Absolutely smashing." The director took her arm and led her toward the makeshift set—three plaster of Paris Corinthian columns arranged in the formal French gardens. "Hand here, my dear. That's my girl." He placed her left hand on one of the columns. "Head . . . like so." He tilted it slightly back so the wind would blow the scarf at her throat. "Do we have enough natural wind?" he yelled. "Do we need the wind machine?"

"Let's try it without." The photographer moved in for a close-up.

"Pouty, my dear. Seductive," the director said. "Look as if you've just made love."

Rose Anne felt the heat that blushed her cheekbones and the tops of her breasts. From under her lashes she glanced back at the tree. Sid was still there, propped against the trunk, watching her.

"That's it! That's perfect!" the director yelled. "Just the look I wanted."

For a moment Sid's dark eyes held her. She was breathless, trembling. Then he turned and walked away.

Calling on her reserves of strength and courage, Rose Anne put personal feelings aside and transformed herself into the Face.

The sound of motorcycles cut through the stillness of the Loire Valley. Sid rode hard and fast, a good half mile in front of his friends. The rich smells of the earth and the lush green of the valley escaped his notice. His eyes were turned inward, to a woman with a face to worship and a body to die for.

He controlled the motorcycle with the same precision and skill he used in the skies. His powerful hands guided the huge machine through the valley and his single-minded concentration kept it on course.

He heard the roar of an engine, and out of the corner of his eye saw Lightning closing in on him. Sid slowed so that Luther could catch up.

Luther motioned toward a copse of trees along the banks of the Loire. Sid nodded, then pulled over.

"What's the rush, Eagle?" Luther brought his machine to a halt, slung his helmet on the handlebars, then stepped off, grinning. "This is supposed to be a sightseeing trip, not a race."

"I feel the need to let off a little steam."

"Don't we all?" Luther sat on the mossy side of a tree and leaned against the trunk. "I'm so keyed up about Saturday, I can hardly think. Tell me again . . . what did she say this morning?"

"She'll go with you."

"You already told me that. What else did she say?"

"She wants to spend some time like ordinary people, Luther. Your job will be to protect her from the crowds, to make damned sure she's not pulled at and fawned over like a prize bone at a dogfight."

"Being the guardian demon again?" Panther, who had just dismounted from his bike, strolled up, munching an apple. "Have one. You look like you could use it." He pulled another from his pocket and handed it to Sid. "An apple a day keeps the doctor away. The head doctor," he added, winking at Luther.

"I don't know why I ever agreed to this crazy plan." Sid slumped against the base of the tree and gazed out over the river.

"Hell, I do." Panther spoke around a big bite of apple. "It's a challenge. You never could resist a challenge."

"With a little bit of blackmail thrown in . . . and friendship." Luther sat down beside Sid. "What's the next step?"

"I'm going to ply her with love letters between now and Saturday, lay the groundwork for you."

He felt like a heel. He really should call the whole thing off before it went too far. Hell, the way he felt about Rose Anne, it had already gone too far. He was going to end up betraying not only Rose Anne and Luther, but himself as well.

"Luther . . ."

"I don't know what I would do with you, Eagle." Luther clapped him on the back. "You're a true friend."

•   •   •

That evening Sid poured out his anguished soul at the piano.

Hearing the music, Rose Anne left her place at the desk, abandoning the letters she was writing, and stole to the balcony. The music was so intense, it brought her to her knees. With her chin propped on her crossed arms, she leaned on the railing, enraptured.

Soon she was so deeply under the musician's spell that she didn't hear her aunt approach.

"I declare. Whoever that is at the piano is plumb obsessed. Come on in. I'm shutting this door." Bitsy reached for the knob.

"No."

"Honey, look what it did to you last night. It tore your insides to pieces."

"I want to hear it, Auntie." Rose Anne looked up at her aunt, totally unaware of the tears on her cheeks. "I *have* to hear it."

Bitsy started to protest, then changed her mind. Shaking her head, she left her niece on the balcony, went to her room, and flicked on the television set. An old Laurel and Hardy film was just the thing for what ailed her . . . whatever that was.

Faint strains of music drifted to her. It had to be a man at the piano. The music was too powerful. Maybe he would quit soon. Or maybe they'd all get lucky and he'd leave Paris, or, at the very least, leave the House of the Angel.

With the last crashing chords still echoing in the air, Sid left the piano and went to the Louis XIV desk. The paper he had bought for the love letters to Rose Anne was heavy bond, cream-colored, plain and simple. He wanted nothing to detract from the words.

Making love to her on paper was easy. Making love to her at the piano was easy.

"Hell, Eagle, you're some kind of hotshot lover and don't even know it," he muttered.

He ripped the paper to shreds and tossed it into the wastebasket, then sat at his desk, staring into space.

Almost, he wished he had never come to Paris. Almost, he wished he had never laid eyes on the Face.

"To live fully is to suffer," he said. He didn't know if he made that up or if he had read it somewhere. No matter. It was true.

He had a vision of Luther clapping him on the back and calling him a true friend. Fixing his mouth into a grim line, Sid picked up a fresh sheet of paper and began to write.

Twenty minutes later he called a bellboy to deliver the love letter to Miss Rose Anne Jones. Then he left his apartment and hurried down the steps, two at a time. Maybe the breezes in the courtyard would clear his head.

Sid leaned against one of the cool stone columns and looked out over the rose garden. For the first time since he'd come to Paris, it failed to soothe his soul. He waited, hoping for a sense of peace to finally steal over him. When it became obvious that he was doomed to torment, he decided to join his buddies.

They had gone back to the nightclub on the Left Bank, Lightning to fill the time until Saturday, Hawk to tell outrageous stories and keep them all laughing, and Panther and Gunslinger to scout for women.

Sid had been foolish to stay behind. Telling them he needed to compose love letters for Luther was merely an excuse. He had stayed behind hoping for a glimpse of Rose Anne.

He glanced up at her lighted window. No one was there.

"I didn't expect to see anyone here."

Rose Anne's voice pierced his heart. He turned around to see her standing beside the bench, a vision of beauty in white. She looked like an angel visiting the garden.

"I like to come down for the night breeze," he said, keeping staunchly at his post.

Rose Anne sat on the bench, and her filmy skirt billowed around her. With one hand she lifted her heavy hair off her neck.

"Ahhh, that feels good."

"Long day?" He could hardly speak. In fact he was surprised he didn't sound like a bullfrog in heat. The sight of that long, lovely neck was almost his undoing.

"The usual." She let her hair drift back down around her shoulders, then smiled at him once more. "It's not the day that has me hot. It's your friend's love letters."

"He makes love well, does he?"

"Yes. Oh, yes." She lifted her hair again, exposing her skin to the kiss of moonbeams. "Are you surprised?"

"Luther's a handsome man."

"How like a man to think a handsome face must necessarily belong to a fool."

"You misunderstand me. Luther is my friend. I'm glad he courts you well."

"It's not his face that impresses me; it's his soul. Such passion, such power."

Sid dared not claim the words. Even if she knew they had come from *his* soul, she would still be taken aback by his face, his nose. He quickly squashed the foolish hopes that leapt to life. A great beauty like Rose Anne deserved a handsome man, one whose looks wouldn't embarrass her in public.

He must continue to play the fool.

"What does he write? Poetry? Great intellectual treatises? Erotica?"

"It's the strangest thing—" Rose Anne paused, as if she were considering whether to confide in him.

"I'm perfectly harmless, a homely father confessor." He grinned. "You can tell me anything."

"I've always had that feeling about you . . . that I can tell you anything. I guess it's because I trust you."

Sid wished the earth would open up and swallow him.

"I don't know if a beautiful woman like you should trust a man with a nose like mine. Remember Pinocchio? He got that nose from telling a bunch of lies."

Rose Anne laughed. Then she patted the bench. "Sit beside me. I need someone to talk to."

"Aunt Bitsy?"

"She's wrapped up in the television set. Old movies. She lives and breathes them . . . when she's not wearing herself out being my girl Friday and my substitute mother." She patted the bench again. "I hate to keep bothering her with my troubles."

"A beautiful woman like you should never have troubles."

Sid slid onto the bench beside her. He wondered if she could hear his heart slamming against his ribs.

"You asked me what he writes?" Rose Anne turned toward him. The slight movement angled her knees against his thigh.

He clenched his jaw against the sudden passion that ripped through him. A man in his condition had no business sitting in a deserted garden with the object of his desire.

But she needed him. What else could he do?

"Sometimes I think it's poetry," she said. "Other times it's wisdom that shows a great understanding of the human condition." She turned her shining face toward the rose garden and quoted the first two lines of the love letter he had so recently written.

"You've commited his words to heart?"

"Every one of them." Her laughter was like morning dew, fresh and sparkling. "I'm afraid he's gotten to me."

"Then he's a master of seduction."

"He's a *god* of seduction." She turned back to him, and even in the moonlight he could see the flush on her cheeks. "It's more than his love letters; it's his music. Talk about erotica."

"His music?"

"I hear it almost every evening. It touches me in ways I've never been touched." She smiled at him. "Is that silly?"

"No. It's romantic . . . if you believe in all that stuff." Sid stood up. He had to break the physical contact with her, for he was dangerously close to telling her the truth.

"Believe in it! Don't tell me you're one of those cynics."

"Seduction with music and poetry. It all sounds excessive to me. Self-indulgent and overblown."

Rose Anne laughed. "I suppose that's what most men would think. But my poet is no ordinary man."

"Then you're in love with him already?"

"I don't know . . . it's crazy. I think I'm in love with his soul."

"The body won't be far behind." He forced himself to grin at her. "Congratulations, Rose Anne. Luther is quite a guy."

"That's what I'm finding out."

"Will you tell him how you feel Saturday?"

"Why . . . no. Until Luther says with his

mouth what he says so beautifully with his pen, I won't tell him anything. If a man can rhapsodize and dream on paper, surely he can do it in person."

"He's shy."

"If he feels half of what he writes, he'll become bold."

"For you, any man would be bold."

She tilted her head and studied him. He endured her scrutiny without flinching.

"I thought you didn't believe in all that poetic stuff," she said, laughing.

"A slip of the tongue. Shall I cut the offending fool off?"

"Oh, please. Not for my sake . . . You've made me laugh so much, I'm going to get a stitch in my side."

"Sewed with black thread or white?"

"You never stop, do you?"

"If I did, I'd catch up to my nose, and then there'd be a terrible collision." He swept his arm out and gave her a grand and exaggerated bow. "Good night, fair lady. Sweet dreams."

"Good night, Sid . . . and thank you."

"For being the court jester?"

"For being you."

Four

Sid tossed in his bed. The courtyard session with Rose Anne had destroyed any hope of sleep. Throwing back the covers, he walked to the window. Her apartment was dark. In fact, most of the apartments were dark.

Barefoot, he padded back to the bedside table. The luminous hands on his watch dial pointed to two o'clock.

Sid walked to the piano and sat down. The music was not for her tonight. It was for him.

His hands moved slowly, lovingly, as if the keyboard were her body, trembling for his touch. Playing softly so as not to disturb his neighbors, he began to make love to Rose Anne.

He skimmed the keys with his fingertips, touching her in secret places. He explored her with exquisite tenderness, lingering over the touch. The treble notes were her nipples, lush and ripe. He played with them until they were a tight melody pulsing under his fingertips.

His hands shivered on the keyboard, the left moving to the bass, to her sweet, exotic curves and her rich, silken hollows. There was instant response to his skillful hands.

Music soared, fiercely erotic and deeply satisfying. He rammed his foot on the soft pedal to muffle the increasing intensity of music. He leaned closer, pouring out his hopeless love.

Across the way the faint strains of music drifted into Rose Anne's consciousness. She came awake slowly, unaware at first of what had disturbed her sleep. Ever so softly, the passionate music crept over her, stealing her breath, bending her will.

Sighing, she cupped her breasts and lay back against the pillow. The music brushed her parted lips in a rush of wings unseen. Transported, she gave herself up, a willing slave to the unknown master, a waiting vessel to his dark fire.

Bitsy sat at the glass-top table, still wearing her pink nightcap. Berries heaped with cream sat in the cereal bowl and the morning paper waited, folded, beside her coffee.

She studied her niece critically when she came through the door. No dark circles, thank goodness.

"Did you sleep well, honey?"

"Hmmm." Rose Anne sat down and poured skim milk over her berries. She had a dreamy, faraway look on her face.

"Another note came for you this morning."

"Another one?"

"Lord knows, I reckon all that man has time to do is write notes." Bitsy handed it to her.

Color flushed Rose Anne's cheeks as she read. Watching, Bitsy worried at her nightcap and fiddled with the silver.

Rose Anne looked up from the note. "Is something wrong, Auntie?"

"That's what I'd like to know."

"Everything's fine." Rose Anne smiled as she

folded the note and tucked it into her bosom. "Just fine."

"I don't know that I'm liking what I'm seeing."

"And what's that?"

"A few notes and a little bit of night music, and you're looking like a woman in love."

"Oh, pooh, Auntie." Rose Anne waved her hand. "I'm not in love." Color flooded her cheeks once more. "At least, I don't think I'm in love. It's just that Luther is such a *nice* man, and his notes and music are—" Rose Anne left her untouched berries and began to pace the floor. "I don't know how to explain it. When I hear him sing or read his poetry, it's almost as if I'm looking straight into his heart. He's so very wise and beautiful."

"You don't know him."

"Because of what he writes, I know him better than I've ever known a man."

"How come he has to keep sending notes? How come he can't say all that in person?"

"He's shy. When he gets accustomed to me, he'll speak up."

"It all sounds fishy to me, like he's got something to hide."

"You sound like Sid. He calls all this excessive, self-indulgent, and overblown."

"Now, there's a sensible man. A bit on the homely side, but then, I never did trust a handsome face. Look what a snake Riker Garvin turned out to be."

Rose Anne sank into her chair, her knees suddenly weak. She hadn't thought of him in months.

"I shudder to think what would have happened if you hadn't found out about him before he got you to the altar."

Rose Anne had found out about him the hard way. Two weeks before the wedding she'd caught him in bed with another woman. The really awful part was that it had been *her* bed. When he'd been caught, Riker had coolly explained that he'd wanted Sylvie to know just what kind of luxuries he'd be able to afford her once he married the Face and her fortune.

"And then, of course, there was the wealthy Mr. Gordon, whose oil wells turned out to be dry holes." Bitsy banged her spoon against the glass table. "Snakes, all of them."

Rose Anne hadn't gotten close to the altar with Mike Gordon, but she had almost lost her heart . . . until she'd discovered that he wanted her to finance his exploratory drilling.

"Luther's not like that. I *know* he isn't."

The anguish in Rose Anne's voice stopped Bitsy's tirade. She left the table and put her arm around her niece.

"Forgive me for being an old fool. It's just that I worry about you."

"You worry too much."

"I know. First I worry that you're going to go on modeling the rest of your life and end up a dried-up old spinster like me, and then I worry that you're going to fall for the wrong man and end up brokenhearted. I'm just a natural worrywart."

"Let's do something to take your mind off my troubles. What's your favorite thing to do in Paris?"

"Well . . ."

"Come on, Auntie. Don't be shy." Rose Anne grabbed her hands, laughing. "Your favorite thing to do in Paris is . . . ?"

"To buy some of that perfume made in Grasse that makes me smell like an expensive madame." Bitsy grinned at her confession.

"Then let's go shopping. We have four hours until that awful luncheon Charlie arranged."

"I think I'll wear the perfume to lunch. Lots of

it." Bitsy pulled off her cap and fluffed her red curls, compliments of a drugstore bottle. "Reckon old Charlie will notice?"

Rose Anne heard the longing in her aunt's voice. She gave her a warm hug.

"We'll make darned sure he does. There's a great beauty salon we're going to and a smashing little dress shop. When I'm finished with you, he'd have to be blind not to notice."

"I don't want him to have a heart attack or anything, just . . . notice me."

Sid was in the bookstore, browsing, and suddenly there she was, the Face, sitting at a small sidewalk café across the street, sipping something, probably lemonade, from a glass that looked as tall and cool as she was. He replaced the book, reaching blindly for the shelf, never taking his eyes off Rose Anne.

She wore a big hat to shade her face from the sun but no sunglasses to hide the brilliant green of her eyes. He leaned closer to the window.

"Can I help you, sir?"

The question was spoken in French, and Sid answered in French . . . with a Kentucky drawl. He was just browsing, he said. He hoped the cute little salesgirl understood.

She did. But she couldn't hide her amusement. Covering her mouth with her hand, she giggled.

The salesclerk vanished and Sid stood at the window, trying to think of a good reason to go across the street and sit beside Rose Anne. The table was small. Their knees and elbows would touch. He would smell her hair, her skin.

If he had anything to write on, he would take her a note from Luther. But how could he explain delivering a note at a sidewalk café?

Across the way she lifted the cool glass and

touched her throat. Sid rammed his fists into his pockets—hard.

A well-dressed man approached her table, seeking her autograph, Sid hoped. The man doffed his hat and stood politely while he talked. Rose Anne's smile was guarded, her manner distant.

Suddenly her smile vanished and her back stiffened. Sid was instantly alert.

The man said something else to her, then sat down at the table. Sid was out the door.

He loped along, craning his neck to see her over the crowd that thronged the sidewalk. She was still at the table, struggling to remain polite but looking increasingly uncomfortable.

Sid pushed through the crowd with as much tact as he could manage. A few people complained of squashed toes, but he hurried on. He didn't have time to think up an apology in French.

When he got close enough, he saw that the man had his thigh pressed intimately against Rose Anne's. She was pressed hard against the back of her chair.

Sid nearly crushed a waiter in his dash to her table.

"Ah, there you are, sis," he said, looming beside them like a giant saguaro cactus. All prickles. "Did you get over your morning sickness?"

Rose Anne smiled with relief. Sid hooked a chair with his big foot and dragged it to the small table. He winked at her, then angled himself between Rose Anne and her unwelcome visitor, stretching his long legs every which way in order to come between the two of them.

"I beg your pardon." The man's English was impeccable, with only a slight French accent. "That's my foot you're stepping on."

"An old habit of mine, stepping on feet." Sid clapped him on the shoulder hard enough to rattle his ribs. "I'm trying to turn over a new leaf, but I just don't know which leaf to turn over." He whacked the astonished man on the back, laughing loudly at his own humor.

"Are you some kind of nut?"

"He's my brother." Rose Anne suddenly clutched her stomach, and Sid would have sworn she turned pale. "I think I'm going to be sick again." Sid grinned as she gagged.

The unwelcome visitor stood up so fast, he almost toppled his chair. "This is all a terrible mistake. I thought she was the Face."

"Lots of people make that mistake when she's sitting down. Don't they, Ruby?" Sid gently poked Rose Anne in the ribs. "You ought to see her standing up. Why, sis's legs are so bowed, you could run a cow between them and still have room left over. Besides that, she's got a big old ugly mole on her midriff. And in a few months, when she starts showing, she's going to get as large as a washtub. All the Granger women do."

The man made a hasty exit, every now and then looking back over his shoulder as if he expected Sid to be pursuing him.

"Bow legs and a mole on my midriff?" Rose Anne said after she had finished laughing.

"A great big ugly one."

They laughed some more.

"Did you see his face when you asked me about morning sickness?"

"He turned three shades of green."

"Big as a washtub, huh?" Rose Anne stood up and frowned down at her twenty-two-inch waistline as if she expected it to have ballooned.

"It sounded like a good idea at the time."

Rose Anne sat back down, propped her elbows on the table, and leaned close to him, her eyes dancing with mischief. He had never seen her look lovelier. At that moment he would gladly have given up the skies for the sake of remaining at her side to bring laughter into her eyes.

"Some men would have taken a different approach," she said, teasing him. "Offered to fight a duel to save my honor."

"Swords at twenty paces. I would have won by a nose."

A breeze caught the brim of her hat when she tipped her head back to laugh. Sid reached up and rescued it as it threatened to sail into the street.

"I don't know what I would have done today without you," she said, straightening her hat. "You've been my knight in shining armor."

Sid tried to keep his extraordinary pleasure hidden. "I thought that was Aunt Bitsy's job. Where is she?"

"Getting gorgeous. I left her in the dress shop with explicit orders not to come out until she's completely transformed." She smiled at him. "Tell me about yourself, Sid."

"I'm just a simple Kentucky boy who got lucky enough to fly Tomcats for the navy."

"In a pig's eye. You're ambitious and hardworking, not lucky."

"In a pig's eye?"

"I'm just a simple Georgia girl who got lucky enough to model for the world's top magazines," she said, mimicking him.

They laughed, and the waiter came by to take orders. They ordered two lemonades.

"So . . . where are your friends?"

"Luther?"

"Yes." Her cheeks flushed. "I'm not going to pretend with you. You see, I've never had a simple, honest friendship with a man before. Somehow my relationships with them always got complicated." She touched his hand. "Your friendship is too important to throw away with pretense and prevarication."

He should end the charade. Now. But if he told

the truth to save one friendship, he would be jeopardizing another. Looking at the problem from all angles, he decided the truth would serve no purpose except to destroy both Rose Anne and Luther's confidence in him.

The truth would set you free, the tiny voice of his conscience told him.

"What's wrong?" she said, squeezing his hand.

"Why do you ask?"

"A sadness came into your eyes."

"It was the thought of you . . . big as a wash-tub. You *do* plan to have children, don't you?"

She smiled. "I love children. I have three lively nephews and two beautiful nieces. Someday I'd like to have some of my own."

"Luther's a handsome man."

"Things certainly haven't gone that far." Color came into her cheeks again, and he remembered his night music and how she had said it seduced her. "And they never will unless he tells me face-to-face all the lovely things he says in his letters."

"He's at the Louvre, by the way."

"He loves art?"

"Yes."

"That figures. He's a poet, a musician. Naturally he would like the visual arts as well."

"Well . . . I don't know that he's all that much of a poet. . . ."

"Oh, Sid." She squeezed his hand, laughing. "Someday you're going to fall in love, and suddenly all the romantic notions you scoff at won't seem silly anymore."

"Ah, love. Another silly notion."

With their hands still joined, they looked at each other. Something moved in her eyes, something bright and full of wonder. Sid held her gaze, basking in it, drowning in it.

The ice in their lemonade glasses melted and fell apart with a pop. And still they stared.

She flicked her tongue over her full bottom lip. Sid's blood pressure went up.

Rose Anne was the first to pull away. Self-consciously, she pressed her hand against her throat.

"It's getting late. I wonder what's keeping Aunt Bitsy?"

"Do you want me to walk with you to the dress shop and see if we can find her?"

"Thank you, but I'm perfectly capable of walking alone."

"What? A woman in your condition! I wouldn't hear of it, sis." He held back her chair, then tucked her arm through his. "Or do you want me to call you Ruby?"

"You're so crazy. Don't ever change." She laughed up at him. "And by the way, when you see Aunt Bitsy, act smitten."

They found Bitsy in the dress shop, gussied up like a Thanksgiving turkey. She had been tucked and squeezed into a girdle and a waist cincher, then cajoled into a stunning designer dress that emphasized her newly streaked red and gold hair.

Sid whistled, then bowed deeply over her hand. "If Ruby here is not careful, you're going to do her out of a job."

"Ruby?" Bitsy Rucker raised a newly plucked eyebrow.

"It's a long story. I'll tell you on the way to lunch." Rose Anne held her hand out to Sid. "Thanks . . . for everything."

"All in a day's rescue, sis." He left the shop, whistling.

"Sis?"

Rose Anne tucked her arm through Bitsy's. "Come on, Auntie. We have lot to talk about."

•   •   •

"You've got to tell her, Luther. Today."

"I don't know if I can." Luther fiddled with his tie. "How do I look, Eagle?"

"Like a man who can be Lightning in a courtship as well as in the skies."

"Oh, hell." Luther ran his hands through his hair, then crossed to the mirror and took Sid's comb to repair the damage.

The two of them were in Sid's apartment, waiting for the arrival of their buddies. The plan was simple. Eagle, Panther, Gunslinger, and Hawk would go to the air show as planned, but Lightning would stay behind to bring the Face. He had suggested they rent a van and all go together, but Panther had hooted at the idea. "You've got to court her in style," he'd said. "By the time you get her to the air show, she should already be falling over you, panting to hop into the sack." One look at Eagle's face had caused him to moderate his advice. "Or into the nearest restaurant for a good steak dinner."

Remembering that conversation, Sid scowled. He didn't know which was going to fall apart first, his temper or the charade. If things didn't break soon, he was going to leave Paris, fly over to Madrid or Naples or even to London. Anywhere would be better than the protracted agony of Paris, of seeing Rose Anne every day, of watching her fall in love with his words, his music . . . and his best friend.

"Do you love her, Luther?"

"I think so."

"You think?"

"You sound like a grizzly bear. What's the matter with you?"

"This charade is not right. It's gone too far. If you love her, tell her so."

"I can't say it the way you can."

"Just say what you feel. If she loves you, pretty words won't matter."

"Well . . . I'll try."

"Good."

"I know I've asked a lot of you, Eagle. Don't think I don't know how hard all this has been on you. You, with all your scruples and high-minded principles."

He didn't know the half of it. Sid hid his turmoil behind a big grin. Luther was his flying buddy, and he would die for him. Almost had, as a matter of fact.

"That's what friends are for." He clasped Luther's shoulder.

Rose Anne was ready for the air show a full thirty minutes before Luther arrived. Her azure blue dress was comfortable and made her feel confident.

"How do I look?" She twirled around the room for Bitsy.

"You've asked me that a dozen times, and I've told you a dozen times. You look astonishingly gorgeous. All of Paris will be watching you instead of the airplanes."

Rose Anne rubbed her hands together. Her palms were moist. Why was she so nervous over a simple date?

Echoes of the dark, passionate music swept through her. Her body tingled and she became breathless. The date wasn't so simple after all.

She jumped when the knock came.

"Wish me luck, Auntie," she whispered as she walked to the door.

"Good luck, honey." Bitsy kissed her cheek. "And I do mean that."

Rose Anne took a deep breath, then opened the door. Luther was standing in the hallway, polite, nice, neat, and handsome—head-turning handsome.

Then why was she standing there, waiting for the earth to move and feeling nothing, not even a tiny tremor. Rose Anne clung to the doorknob, waiting for the shock waves to hit. His poetry and his music tumbled through her mind, but even the memories of that couldn't stir her.

Perhaps she was merely tired. The luncheon the day before had been exceedingly tiresome. If it hadn't been for watching Charlie do a double take over Bitsy, and Bitsy flirting with Charlie, Rose Anne couldn't have endured it.

"Hello," Luther said.

"Won't you come in?" Rose Anne held the door wide. Maybe when he passed through she'd suffocate from his body heat.

"Well . . . I guess we ought to be going."

"All right, then. I'll be right back."

She'd stepped out on the balcony earlier and had felt a nip in the air. She got her jacket, stopped long enough to kiss Bitsy's cheek, then joined Luther.

He had rented a Jaguar for the day. It was the sort of extravagant, romantic gesture she might have expected from him. But even inside the snazzy little car, the earth still didn't move.

"You're beautiful," he said.

"Thank you."

"I guess I already said that once."

"No, you haven't."

"Well . . . you're beautiful."

Rose Anne's heart sank. From Luther she expected poetry, rhapsodies. Of course, she hadn't done all that well in the conversation department herself. She tried again.

"Tell me about your work, Luther. About flying."

"It's nice."

"Your friends call you Lightning, I believe."

"Yes."

She sat on her side of the car and watched tourists out the window.

Luther drove, staring straight ahead as if he expected to run into enemy territory at any minute. Dancing with him had been so easy. Especially after that lovely note he'd sent to her table. But then, they hadn't been required to talk.

Maybe he had a note in his pocket. Maybe he'd run to the rest room and memorize it after he parked the car. Then he'd spend the rest of the day dazzling her with his golden tongue.

She sighed. She was being silly. Expecting too much. Wasn't that what Sid had called love and romance? A silly notion?

The thought of him made her smile.

"Is Sid already at the air show?" she asked.

"Yes."

"He says that men who love flying never get far from the skies."

"Yes."

"Tell me what it feels like, being up there in control of such a powerful machine."

"It's . . . uh . . . very nice."

Where were all the lyrical words? Where was that mellifluous voice? Luther's voice bore no resemblance to the magnificent voice she'd heard lifted in song night after night. Maybe a transformation occurred when he sat down at the piano. Maybe she should have packed a piano.

She was being petty and critical. To make up for it, she moved across the seat and linked her hand through his arm.

He almost sideswiped a car in the neighboring lane. After he straightened out the wheel, he grinned sheepishly at her.

"Sorry. It's just . . . you're so damned beautiful."

"Thank you."

Moving back to her side of the car, she sighed. Romantic love had been dealt a severe blow. In fact, it was in dire need of resuscitation.

Maybe a miracle would happen at the air show.

Five

The crowd at the Paris Air Show was in a holiday mood. Rose Anne found it catching. The roar of jets filled the skies and the roar of the crowd filled the air. Bright dresses and bright laughter competed with each other for attention.

Hanging on to Luther's arm, Rose Anne craned her neck, trying to see everything at once.

"It's marvelous," she said.

"Yes, it is. This is one of the reasons I love coming to Paris."

At last Luther was opening up. Her hopes soared.

"Oh, look. There's Sid."

Although he was too far away to have heard her, he turned just as she spoke. She waved and started to call out a greeting to him, but the words died in her throat. Everything she had been waiting for happened all at once. The earth moved, sending shock wave after shock wave rippling through her. She curled her toes in her shoes.

She and Luther moved inexorably closer to Sid.

"Careful, Rose Anne," Luther said.

If she hadn't been holding on to him, she would have fallen.

Sid's gaze held hers. Somewhere up in the skies the pilots were executing a daring move. The spectators craned their necks, sighing a collective gasp as the daring stunt was completed. Sid and Rose Anne saw only each other.

She was breathless by the time she and Luther arrived at their seats.

"And how is the fair Ruby today?" Sid leaned close and whispered in her ear. "No morning sickness?"

"With my protective brother nearby? Not a chance."

Sid leaned around her to shake Luther's hand. When his shoulder touched her arm she felt the shock waves again.

This is ridiculous, she told herself. She turned staunchly toward Luther and began asking him every question she could think of about the planes and the pilots to get him talking, to get her attention off Sid, to make her forget the way he made her skin tingle and her breath short and her heart thump too fast.

It was a valiant effort, but it didn't work. All her senses were attuned to Sid. She felt as if a giant magnet were centered in him, pulling at her so hard, she thought she would end up wrapped around him. She felt giddy and anxious, happy and unaccountably sad.

She gave up all efforts to engage Luther in conversation and settled back to ponder her dilemma. Sid was warm and friendly and funny, but it was Luther she longed for, Luther who made the dark fire burn through her at night.

Over the loudspeaker came the announcement that an experimental jet was next in the skies. A hush fell over the crowd.

Rose Anne felt Sid tense. She watched him covertly, as if she were the secret police of some exotic foreign country and he had the key to world destruction. Every muscle in his powerful body was geared for flight. His right hand curved around an invisible stick. The gesture was that of both lover and master. He caressed and commanded at the same time. His face was tight, full of anticipation, excitement, and passion.

There was a roar from the jet and a roar from the crowd. Sid was transported to another dimension . . . and Rose Anne along with him.

He lifted his face to the sun, and all the wonders of the skies shone in his eyes. Rose Anne flew with him to a world wide and clean, a world far above the petty strivings of man, a world of such beauty, such grandeur, she held her breath lest it vanish.

Time spun away like golden filaments on a dew-sparkled spider's web. Even the breeze stood still while Rose Anne secretly watched the glory of flight. Sid's left hand shaded his eyes, while his right hand guided the plane, moving the invisible stick.

From somewhere deep inside her, haunting music stirred. The strains, faint at first, soon became a symphony.

She turned her head quickly toward Luther, expecting to feel the impact of the man and the music, blended together in one glorious moment. All she felt was admiration for a handsome, noble, and very nice man.

On her left the magnetic pull of Sid's presence drew her back. Far above them the experimental jet was a silver dot, and all around, the crowd waited and watched, breathless.

In the sunlit silence Sid was as still as a carving, the yearning so clear in his face, it hurt to look. And yet she couldn't do otherwise, for she was lost in his passion, lost in the bright visceral moment as he chased his secret vision of glory.

When the plane vanished over the horizon and

there was nothing left to see except an endless summer sky, Rose Anne sighed.

Sid turned to her. Leaning close, he placed one finger on her left cheek. "Tears?" he whispered, his voice as gentle as his touch.

"Beauty always makes me cry." She reached into the pocket of her jacket and pulled out a lace-edged handkerchief. She dried her tears without shame, smiling at him all the while.

It was at that precise moment, with the sun shining in her eyes and tears glistening on her cheeks, that Sid realized the enormity of his love. When he had first glimpsed her through the garden gate, he had been taken by her grace and her beauty. Later he had fallen under the spell of her charm. Now it was the purity of her soul that beckoned to him.

His love was so great, he would die for her. And yet, she belonged to another.

Out of the corner of his eye he glanced toward Luther—innocent, trusting Luther. His best friend.

"Would you excuse me, please?" Sid stood up.

"Hey, Eagle." Luther turned to him, smiling. "What's up?"

"I'm leaving."

"Leaving the air show?" Disbelief showed in Luther's face and his voice.

"Not the show. Just these seats. I'm tired of sitting." Sid glanced down at Rose Anne. Her eyes were still bright with the remnants of unshed tears. If he didn't get out of there soon, he would surely make a fool of himself.

"You're going?" she whispered.

He opened his mouth to make excuses, but the lie caught in his throat. All he could do was nod.

She touched his arm. "Good-bye . . . and thanks." He lifted one eyebrow. "For making me see the beauty."

"You're welcome, fair lady."

He hurried away before he was tempted to change his mind. Panther and Gunslinger left their seats and followed him.

"What's up, Eagle?" Panther asked.

He started to repeat the lie he'd told Luther, then changed his mind.

"It's this damned courtship thing. I can't sit there and watch it. I feel like a cheat and a liar."

"I've got a simple solution to your problem." Gunslinger fell into step on Eagle's left side. "What you need is a woman."

"Damned straight, that's what he needs," Panther said. "He's spent so much time courting Luther's woman, he hasn't had time to win one for himself."

"One phone call will fix that. Panther and I have met some women . . . oo-la-la."

"Yeah. Let's call them up and ask them to come down and meet us."

Sid started to decline, then changed his mind. No use drowning in a sea of self-pity.

"Okay. Let's give them a call."

They found a phone booth at the entrance to the air show. While Panther made the call, Eagle and Gunslinger looked up at the skies, watching the show.

"Do you think he'll tell her today?" Eagle asked.

"Will who tell who what?"

"Luther. Will he tell Rose Anne he loves her?"

"He's planning to, but I wouldn't place money on it."

"Why not?"

"For one thing, I don't think he'll get up the courage, and for another, I don't think he really loves her."

Wild hope sprang up in Sid's breast. "What makes you think that?"

"I don't know. A hunch. I think he's just star-struck. I'm a little bit that way around her myself. After all, she *is* the most beautiful woman in the world."

"She's the sun, and other women mere shadows."

Gunslinger gave him a funny look. "Hell, Eagle, if I didn't know better, I'd say you were in love with her."

"Does an ordinary frog aspire to be Prince Charming?"

"Aw, hell. You and your poetry. Let's go and see if Panther reached the women."

After Sid left, the air show seemed endless. Rose Anne tried to muster her interest, but it kept flagging. About lunchtime Luther got up enough courage to reach for her hand. She smiled politely, but her heart wasn't in it. Her heart wasn't in anything. It seemed to have gone on leave the minute Sid had said good-bye.

By midafternoon she pleaded fatigue, and Luther drove her back to the apartments. In the hallway he leaned down and kissed her. The kiss was pleasant, even fairly expert, but she felt as if she were kissing one of her brothers.

Something was terribly wrong.

"Luther," she said, pushing away from him.

"Yes?"

"Would you come inside and play something for me. I have a piano in the apartment."

"Play something?"

He looked as if she had asked him to commit murder.

"Or come inside and sit at my desk and write one of your beautiful love poems while I make us some lemonade."

"I . . . uh." He ran his finger around his collar. "My . . . uh . . . muse has deserted me. Maybe another time . . . tonight. That's it. Tonight. You stand on the balcony and I'll play."

"I would love to see you play. May I come to your apartment and watch?"

"Well, uh . . . I got it. You stand on your balcony and I'll stand underneath and . . . uh, sing or something like that."

Rose Anne studied him. He was incredibly handsome and incredibly earnest. Maybe tonight would bring the magic. And then when he kissed her, sparks would fly and she would burn.

"All right, Luther." She caressed his cheek. "Thank you for a lovely day."

"You're welcome."

"You told her *what*?"

Sid paced his apartment like a wild animal spoiling for a kill. Gunslinger, Panther, and Hawk were chuckling into their beers, while Lightning stood apart, looking sheepish and running his hands through his hair. The pizza they had ordered for dinner sat cooling in the cardboard boxes.

"It sounds like a good idea to me." Panther hooted as he reached for the pizza.

"Yeah, Eagle," Gunslinger added. "You caterwauling under her balcony while Lightning stands in the moonlight, moving his mouth and looking handsome. It ought to work." He slapped his thigh and doubled over laughing.

"I won't do it. This has gone far enough." Sid scowled at Luther. "If you love her, get over there and tell her the truth and put an end to all these lies."

"Do this one last thing for me, and I won't ask you for any more, Eagle."

"Do it, Eagle," Hawk said. "You ought to be

feeling generous. Panther says you scored big with Janine today."

"She batted her eyelashes for two hours and pinched my butt twice." Sid scowled at all of them. "Some score."

In high spirits, the pilots sipped beer and ate pizza and cajoled Sid. Finally he gave in.

"This is the way we'll do it . . ." He put his arm around Luther's shoulders and told him the plan.

Panther, Hawk, and Gunslinger, ever resourceful, found a cheap guitar at an all-night pawn shop. Then they gathered on the dark balcony of Sid's apartment to watch the show.

"I'm nervous." Luther stood in the moonlit courtyard just outside Rose Anne's balcony, the cheap guitar strapped around his shoulders.

"You ought to be. I'm thinking of all the ways I'm going to make you suffer before I kill you." Sid hid in the shadows of the rose trellis underneath the balcony.

"Let's get on with it while there are still lights in her window."

"All right. Put your hands on the guitar like I told you . . . the left hand a little higher . . . that's it." Sid strummed a chord on his own guitar. As always, the sound of music soothed him. "Don't forget to move your hands *and* your mouth," he said softly. "Ready?"

"Ready."

The first strains of guitar music brought Rose Anne out of her seat.

"That's him, Auntie."

"How do you know? I thought he played the piano."

"The music is the same." She pressed her hands over her heart. "Listen."

Bitsy rolled her eyes. "The saints preserve us."

Rose Anne's eyes danced as she hurried toward the balcony. "Do you want to come?"

"Lordy, no. I'll just go sit by the television and pretend I'm in Hollywood."

Bitsy left for her room, and Rose Anne pushed open the French doors.

Rose Anne stood at the balcony railing. "Luther?" she called softly.

"Rose Anne."

She had imagined the sound of her name on his lips would thrill her, especially since it was enhanced by his music, but the thrill didn't come. She leaned over the railing so she could see him, strumming the guitar in the moonlight.

As always, the haunting chords seduced her. She began to sway with the beat.

Luther opened his mouth, and the magnificent voice she had heard only from afar rose from beneath her balcony. She was amazed at the difference between Luther's speaking voice and his singing voice. It was the difference between mild breezes and raging typhoons, between curving hillsides and craggy mountains.

Suddenly she saw a vision of Sid at the air show, a vision of such intensity, she was almost blinded. Rose Anne closed her eyes and let the music transport her to another realm.

It was the magic she had been waiting for, the miracle she had longed for, the passion she would die for. Music and moonlight became one, centering its brightness inside her heart.

And when the last chords died away, she stood trembling at the balcony railing.

"You are beautiful, Rose Anne."

Luther's voice shattered the spell. She opened

her eyes. With his face uptilted, he was ruinously gorgeous.

She sighed. "Rhapsodize for me, Luther. Wax poetic. Gather your dreams into words and send them flying up here to me."

"You are more beautiful than . . . my mother."

"Hmmm. And?"

"And . . . and . . . all my sisters put together."

Behind the rose trellises, Sid groaned.

"What did you say, Luther?"

"Tell her you love her," Sid whispered.

"I can't."

Rose Anne leaned over the railing. "You can't what, Luther?"

"Uh . . . rhapsodize."

"Yes, you can. You do it in your notes all the time. You sang in the dark. Now make love to me in the dark with beautiful words."

Sid cursed softly in the darkness. Then he whispered to Luther, "Repeat after me, Lightning . . . Lightning?"

"Okay."

"Come fall with me beneath this summer sky/ And feel the grasses bending with our haste," Sid whispered.

Luther spoke the words hesitantly. He looked miserable, the guitar hanging forlornly around his neck.

"To catch this . . . fleeting world . . . in Love's embrace;/And cling . . . to this sweet day . . . before it dies," Luther mumbled, trying not to stumble over Sid's words and struggling with the unfamiliar rhythm of the sonnet.

"Luther?" Rose Anne called down from the balcony. "Is something wrong?"

"Uh . . . no . . . why?"

"You speak so haltingly."

There was dead silence beneath the balcony.

Sid scowled into the dark, and Luther squeezed the neck of his newly acquired guitar.

"Come, Luther," Rose Anne coaxed. "Be eloquent. Let your voice match your words."

"Damn," Sid said.

"What was that, Luther?"

"What?" he asked.

"I thought I heard a noise under the balcony."

"Uh . . . it was just me sneezing." Luther exaggerated a huge sneeze. He pulled the strap of the guitar over his shoulder. "I guess I'd better be going."

"Oh, please. Not until you finish. Would you leave me clinging to the sweet day before it dies?"

"Come spin with me upon a swirling stream," a powerful voice said as a long arm hooked Luther and dragged him out of sight under the balcony. "Not a word," Sid whispered. "And fall away with me in time and space," he continued. "Then slow this world to our own measured pace/The slow but frenzied pace of Lovers' dreams."

"Ah. That's more like it." Rose Anne peered into the darkness. "Your voice grows stronger."

"Come dance with me for day's end can't be far;/ And sing with me to push aside our fears:/ Our terror of the cruel and countless years/That lean above us with the night's first stars."

"That's hauntingly beautiful," Rose Anne said. "I feel tears on my face."

"Don't cry, fair lady." Forgetting the words he was saying were for Luther, Sid pressed his hand over his heart and spoke the final lines of the sonnet straight from his soul.

"Come love me now beneath this parting sky/ And cherish this sweet day before it dies."

"Yes," Rose Anne said. "Yes . . . I'm coming down."

"No!" Sid all but yelled his protest.

Luther clutched his stomach and groaned. "I think I'm going to be sick."

"What's going on down there?" Rose Anne strained her eyes into the night, trying to see. "Come out from under the balcony so I can see you, Luther."

"What do I do now?" Luther whispered.

"Shut up and keep quiet." Sid told Luther as he tried to think his way out of the dilemma. "I cherish the cloak of darkness, for I am shadow and you are light."

"Beautiful words, but still I want to see you."

"How could any man dare be so bold as to court you openly. Therefore, I hide behind phrases and rose trellises underneath your balcony."

"Luther?" Rose Anne moved to the edge of the balcony and leaned far over, trying to see from another angle. "You don't sound like yourself. Why is your voice hesitant one minute and bold and strong the next? You sound like . . ." Suddenly the truth dawned on Rose Anne. "Sid Granger!"

"The jig's up," Luther said, groaning.

"Hell," Sid said.

"Come out from there. Both of you." Rose Anne was red with rage.

"This is not what you think," Sid said, stepping out from under the balcony. For Luther's sake he was sorry the plan hadn't worked, but for his own, he was glad it was over.

"How could you possibly know what I think? Or why do you even pretend to care?"

"I care." Sid stood tall in the moonlight, looking straight up into her face. "I care more than you'll ever know."

Her heart bumped hard against her ribs, and even in the midst of her rage she felt the passion.

"Damn you to hell," she said softly, tears streaming down her cheeks.

"Rose Anne," Luther said, stepping out from underneath the balcony, his guitar hanging crooked and his cheek scratched from a rose thorn. "Please, Rose Anne."

Rose Anne turned her anger toward him. "I don't ever want to see you again as long as I live. . . . Either of you," she added, whirling toward Sid.

"I'm sorry, Rose Anne," Luther said. "I didn't mean—"

"Leave," she said.

With his guitar banging against his legs, Luther left. But Sid stood before her balcony. He had to make amends.

"He loves you, Rose Anne. He asked me to court you for him only because he's too shy to say the things he feels."

"How do I know what he feels? I know only how I feel . . . how the poems and the music made me feel."

"It's all true. Everything I wrote, every note I played. All of it was for you."

"For Luther, you mean. And for you." She wiped her cheeks with the backs of her hands. "I was just a pawn in your sick game."

"It started as a bet—"

"A bet!"

"But it was never a game. Never."

"Why should I believe you? Nothing you've ever said to me has been true."

"I lied about the notes and the music, Rose Anne. But only because Luther is my friend. He loves you. And I thought you would love him because he's so handsome."

"Do you think I'm that shallow? That nothing matters to me except the way a person looks?"

The truth hurt. Sid hadn't thought of her as shallow, but he had certainly believed that looks would be important to her.

She took his silence for consent.

"Damn you to hell, Sid Granger. Damn you."

"I'm so sorry, Rose Anne. I never meant to hurt you. I only meant to help Luther . . . and you."

"You made me fall in love . . ."

"With Luther?"

"With a phantom, a dream, a man who never existed except in the dark." Rose Anne took one last look at the anguished man standing beneath her balcony. Confusing emotions ripped at her, passion and romantic love, anger and betrayal.

She whirled to leave the balcony.

"Rose Anne. Wait."

She halted, for the voice that had kept her awake in the dark wouldn't be denied.

"Let me come up and explain," he said.

Even now, even with her heart raw and hurting he had the power to make her want him. Clenching her fists, she stalked to the railing and leaned over.

"I wouldn't let you near me if you were the last man on earth."

The French doors rattled on their hinges as she stormed into her apartment.

Sid stood in the dark with nothing to comfort him except his guitar. He felt like breaking it into a million pieces.

Six

Panther, Hawk, Gunslinger, and Lightning were waiting for Sid when he got back to his apartment. He flung his guitar into the closet and sank onto the sofa.

"One smart remark, and all of you will go home in body casts."

"Hey, don't look at me." Panther held up his hands. "It was going great until old Lightning started telling her how beautiful she was. I thought he was going to compare her to this bird dog next." He doubled over, laughing.

Hawk and Gunslinger joined in, and before long Luther was laughing with them. Only Sid didn't see the humor. He scowled at all of them, trying to cover his own heartbreak with anger.

He had lost all hope now. Not that he'd ever had a chance with her in the first place.

"Hey, Eagle," Luther said. "Don't be so glum. I'm kind of relieved everything worked out this way, if you want to know the truth."

"Relieved? *Relieved!*" Sid stalked around the room, stopping at the window every time he passed it to see if he could catch a glimpse of Rose

Anne. "We went through this whole damned charade for nothing?"

"Well . . . not for nothing, exactly. At first I
thought I loved her. I really did. But then, all she
could talk about was your notes and your music,
and when I brought her home from the air show
and kissed her—"

"You kissed her?"

"Hell, Eagle. That's what people do when they
think they're in love." Panther pulled a cold piece
of pizza loose from the box and stuffed it in his
mouth. "That's what people do even when they're
not in love. Right, Gunslinger?" he said between
bites.

"Yeah, Eagle," Gunslinger said. "You act like
kissing the Face is a major crime."

"Her name is Rose Anne." Sid sprawled on the
sofa and propped his long legs on the table. "And
what we did to her was inexcusable. We hurt her."

"I don't think she's all that torn up over losing
me," Luther said. "Like I said, kissing her was
about the same as kissing one of my sisters. I
thought the sparks might fly if I went through
with the balcony routine, but I was wrong. I guess
love just wasn't in the cards for us."

You made me fall in love, she had said. Sid sat
on the sofa, remembering.

He turned to Luther. "You don't love her, then?"

"No. It was a nice dream, an infatuation . . .
but not love."

Trying to hide his elation, Sid shook the empty
pizza box. "Hey, I'm starving. Who ate all the
pizza?"

Across the way, Bitsy was talking on the phone.
"I don't care if her shoot tomorrow is with
Gabriel and all his angels. Cancel it."

"At this time of night?" Charlie said on the other end of the line. "You know we can't do that."

"Well, then, first thing in the morning."

"What can I tell them?"

"Tell him anything you want." Bitsy paused long enough to glance at Rose Anne, how was sitting pale and dry-eyed in the chair, staring toward the dark balcony. "Just do it."

"In all her years she's missed a shoot only once, and that was when she had the flu."

"This will make twice."

"I'm coming over."

Bitsy started to protest, then changed her mind. "You do that, Charlie. We need to talk."

The next morning Sid's friends rented a Peugeot and set out sightseeing. He stayed behind. When they asked him why, he told them simply, "I have to see Rose Anne." No one dared question him.

In his apartment he wrote her a note in the same poetic language as all the others. Then he tore it to pieces and started over. The note he finally sent to her was a straightforward message asking to see her. It was returned unopened.

"She's no longer there, monsieur," the messenger boy told him.

"No longer there?"

"In that apartment. They checked out this morning."

Sid spent three days searching for her. She seemed to have vanished off the planet. While his friends were smelling the grapes of Bordeaux, he was tracking down leads. While they were viewing the ancient Roman ruins of Provence, he was searching the sidewalk cafés and the ritzy boutiques, looking for the face that haunted his dreams.

He finally located her through sheer luck. In desperation he contacted the press. Jean Pierre Chevalier, who had covered the war in the Gulf, was at his desk. He remembered Eagle Granger, and was willing to help.

Using his clout and his powers of persuasion, Jean Pierre found an enterprising reporter who had sniffed out the whereabouts of the Face.

Sid packed the last of his belongings and zipped his bag. His friends sat in solemn silence on the sofa and two chairs.

"I'm headed to Africa," he said.

When Sid made his announcement, they looked at one another, dumbfounded. Panther was the one to recover.

"Why, Eagle? What in the hell is in Africa that you can't find in Paris?"

"Rose Anne," Sid told them simply.

His friends exchanged shocked glances, as if Sid had announced that he was giving up flying for snake charming.

"I have to find her and make her understand that I never meant to hurt her," Sid said.

"Well, knock me down with a feather. You're going all the way to Africa to apologize to a woman?" This from Gunslinger, who weighed at least two hundred pounds, all of it solid muscle.

"Actually, I just said that to throw you off the scent," Sid said. "My real mission in Africa is to sniff out pleasure and indulge myself up to the snout as long as I don't have to pay through the nose."

The laughter eased the tension. Sid's friends didn't ask for explanations, and wisely didn't tease. One by one they came to him and wished him luck.

Rose Anne was in South Africa, ahead of schedule. The line of exotic clothing would later be shot among the ancient ruins of Zimbabwe and the magnificent Victoria Falls. She and her entourage were camped along the Zambezi River.

The heat was oppressive during the day. Only at night when the sun went down was there some relief. Rose Anne chose the late evenings to walk. She never went far, only around the bend and out of sight of the camp. Alone in the solemn splendor of the sunset and the deep quiet of the vast primitive land, she sought healing.

As she stood by the river, a slight and welcome breeze ruffled her hair and caught her skirts, swirling them around her ankles. She stood quietly, praying that the great distance she had put between herself and Sid would take the edge off her pain.

Out of the stillness came a droning noise, faint at first, like a giant mosquito, then louder and more insistent. She lifted her head toward the sky and saw the plane, its wings glinting red gold in the sunset.

Rose Anne shaded her eyes as the plane came closer. It was descending like a graceful bird. Her pulse began to throb and her breath got short.

"Sid," she whispered.

But that was impossible. He was in Paris.

With her heart hammering, she watched the plane. It glided into the sunset, as if the pilot were making love to the skies. One wing dipped toward her, then the plane set down on grasslands beyond the river, its props stirring the air.

Anticipation beat through Rose Anne like native

drums. She pressed her hand over her heart, waiting.

A tall man stepped from the plane and removed his helmet. Sid Granger.

They stared at each other, two people who had unexpectedly stumbled upon treasure and couldn't yet comprehend the enormity of their wealth.

Run, Rose Anne's mind said to her, while her heart said stay.

With his helmet dangling from one hand, Sid strode toward her. She wound her hands tightly together against the passion that coiled inside her . . . and the pain.

"Rose Anne," he said when he was so close that she could see the night darkness of his eyes.

Her name was like music on his lips. The wild wanting he always evoked in her started all over again.

"How did you find me?" she asked, fighting for control.

"Detective work and determination."

"Why did you come?"

He studied her without replying. Insects beat their wings upon the air and the sun spread its glory across the waters of the river. Rose Anne struggled for breath and composure.

Say something, her mind screamed.

Sid's black eyes seemed to devour her. He towered over her, full of mysterious power and dark passion, tugging at her emotions until she wanted to drop to her knees, begging.

"Because I can't bear to lose you," he whispered.

She sucked in a sharp breath. She had expected him to say many things, but never that.

"What is this? Another of your games?" She took a step backward in order to open the distance between them. "How much money is riding on this bet?"

He didn't say anything, but kept looking at her with sad, dark eyes.

"What's the bet?" she asked. "That I'll be so lonesome in this godforsaken land, I'll take you into my tent? That I'll take you into my bed?"

"Rose Anne . . . don't."

"Don't what? Be realistic?" She pushed at hair that curled damply around her face. "You and Luther taught me realism."

"I'll never forgive myself for that."

"Come now, Sid. A cynic like you? Never forgiving oneself is a romantic notion. And you don't believe in romance."

A look of great pain came onto his face. Rose Anne wavered, almost relented.

But she had been hurt. She wanted to punish.

"Or was that another of your lies?"

"If I had revealed my romantic soul to you, you might have guessed that I was the one who wrote those notes and composed that music."

She could feel his body heat, and the remembered strains of music washed over her. She swayed, her legs suddenly weak.

Sid caught her shoulders.

"Rose Anne?" He leaned toward her, and his breath stirred the tendrils at her cheek. "Are you all right?"

She had never known a man's touch could be so powerful. She struggled against her feelings, but her body betrayed her. She was tight and hot and liquid for him, and her thin blouse left nothing to the imagination.

His gaze seared her skin. She felt as if she were being absorbed by his eyes.

He knew.

Rose Anne groaned.

Suddenly his mouth was on hers. It wasn't a kiss so much as a joining of hearts, of souls. His arms circled her, and he held her with exquisite tenderness.

She tried to be stiff and unresponsive, but she might as well have been battling the wind. How could she not respond when his lips were the maestro and hers the instrument? How could she pull away when he was the sun and the rain and she was the earth, waiting for the infusion of life?

She stood shamelessly in the circle of his arms, craving everything his lips promised, wanting everything his body demanded. Her skirt was gauze, and she could feel the size of him, the hardness of him.

Sid brought out the primitive in her. Even while she told herself to back away, her fingers curled and dug into his skin through his shirt. She felt like a wild animal, a jungle she-cat clawing at her mate.

Never had she known such unbridled passion, not even with Riker Garvin, whom she had pledged to marry. The intensity of her feelings made her weak and mindless. She wanted to sink down into the grasses beside the river. She wanted to strip naked and plunge herself into the water and the mud and draw Sid into her. She wanted to love him in a hundred delicious ways and have him respond with a hundred and one.

Passion ruled her. She was reckless and wanton . . . and totally without memory. For her, nothing existed except the moment and the reality of Sid, pressed so close to her, their bodies felt like one.

She clung to him, praying desperately that she could recapture one tiny shred of control, just enough to push him away before it was too late.

Abruptly, he released her. She swayed like a willow in the wind. Sid steadied her.

She wouldn't be seduced by his hands again. She shrugged them off and stepped back.

"That's an interesting technique, Sid, but it won't work." She hoped he didn't see the lie in her eyes.

"I'm sorry, Rose Anne. I didn't mean to do that."

"Everything you have done has been carefully calculated."

"I came here to apologize."

"For yourself or for Luther?" She scored with her attack. Sid's face tightened with something that looked like pain. He was not only a poet, a musician, and a superb lover, but he was also a good actor.

Sid's wonderful ability to hide his duplicity renewed her anger. "You can fly back to Paris and tell Luther that it's all over. That it never even started . . . And while you're at it, tell him he'd better send another emissary to do his kissing for him."

Sid's dark eyes pierced straight through that lie. But Rose Anne stood firm.

"This is not about Luther, it's about us."

"Us? There is no *us*. There never was."

"We were friends."

"Friends are people you can trust. I don't trust you anymore."

Sid died a little inside. Once he had been her knight in shining armor. He remembered the laughter in her eyes when he had called her Ruby. He remembered the tears on her cheeks when she had thanked him for showing her the beauty of flight.

"You have every right to be angry, Rose Anne."

"You bet I do."

"If you will let me explain my motives . . ."

"I'm an expert on motives, Sid. You see, men have played games with me before. And I've discovered that they're all after something. What are you after?"

Her question caught him off guard. What was he

after? What had sent him chasing all the way to
Africa? He had told himself he had to apologize, to
make her understand, to make amends for hurting her.

She stood facing him with the last rays of sun
turning her eyes to emerald, and he knew that he
hadn't flown across the continent merely to rekin-
dle a friendship. He stood before her, mute,
guarding his hopeless love like a hungry lion
guarding his kill.

Rose Anne whirled to leave. But not before Sid
saw the way she shut down. The light left her eyes;
the animation left her face. Even the life seemed to
leave her body. Her movements were stiff and
robotic as she walked away from him.

"Rose Anne! Wait."

She kept on walking.

"Please . . ."

She never broke stride. Sid stood beside the
river, listening to the mournful murmur of the
water as he watched the woman he loved walk out
of his life.

Anguish clawed at his heart and remorse filled
his soul. As Rose Anne vanished around the bend,
all the light suddenly left the world. A bleak
darkness settled over the land. Sid welcomed it.
He reveled in it. He could mourn in the dark and
no one would see, no one would hear.

"Rose Anne," he whispered, and the river
caught her name and carried it off into the night.

He wasn't aware of the passing of time. He knew
only that finally he was still, as if he had been
turned to stone and left by the river to remind
other lovers of his great folly.

Lieutenant Commander Sid Granger, with his
face like a hatchet and his nose like an eagle's
beak, had dared to love the most beautiful woman
in the world.

Sid shook his fist to the dark skies, then got his gear from the plane and prepared to set up camp.

Bitsy looked up when Rose Anne walked back into camp.

"What took you so long, honey? I was beginning to worry about you."

"You always do." Rose Anne forced herself to smile. She didn't want to tell Bitsy about Sid. Not yet, anyhow. The memory of his kiss still burned through her, and it was far too private to share.

"Are you hungry?" Bitsy held out a platter of sandwiches.

"No . . . thank you." She studied her aunt in the dim glow of lanterns. Bitsy's eyes were unusually bright, her cheeks unusually pink. "Why don't you sit down and rest? You look flushed."

"Oh, it's not the heat." Bitsy fanned herself with her hand as her glance slid in the direction of Charlie's tent. He was sitting in a camp chair in the circle of lantern light, training a flashlight on the pages of a book. Charlie was always reading.

"What's he reading this time?" Rose Anne asked.

Bitsy's cheeks got even brighter. "Romance."

"Romance?"

"He says it's strictly literary curiosity, but I think he's just trying to find out how to court."

"How to court?"

"Are you feeling all right, honey? It's not like you to repeat everything I say."

Rose Anne glanced back over her shoulder as if she expected Sid to appear at any moment. She shivered at the thought—not with fear but with passion. Bitsy didn't miss a thing.

"I knew it would happen. You've gone and gotten yourself sick." She put her hand on Rose Anne's forehead. "Dragging around from pillar to post. Africa, my hind foot. Wait till I get hold of Charlie."

"I'm not sick, Auntie. It's just that—"

A sudden racket in the darkness interrupted her.

"My Lord in heaven," Bitsy said. "What's that?"

They held onto each other, listening. Even Charlie, who could sit in the eye of a hurricane and never lose his place in a book, roused himself out of his chair and came to see what the ruckus was.

He hovered behind Bitsy, clutching her arm, until he remembered that he was the man of the camp, if you didn't count the natives, and that Jim Buck Bushland, who had just finished off a gang of cutthroats singlehandedly and won the lady besides, would never do such a thing as hide behind a lady's skirts.

"Who goes there?" he bellowed, thinking he sounded pretty authoritative and even a little bit heroic.

"It's me," a deep voice bellowed back. "Lieutenant Commander Sid Granger. I'm setting up camp." He sounded as if he were giving commands to a bunch of disorderly ensigns.

"Sid?" Rose Anne had imagined he'd be in his plane, winging his way back to Paris by now. But then, a man who would follow her to Africa in the first place was not the kind of man to give up easily.

"Lieutenant Commander Sid Granger?" Charlie turned to Rose Anne. "The navy followed you to Africa?"

"Not the navy. Just one man."

"The one man you left Paris over?"

"Yes, Charlie."

Charlie pulled a silk plaid handkerchief out of his pocket and wiped his face. He hated controversy. And now it was staring him straight in the face, and he was going to have to do something about it . . . or else lose ground in his blossoming romance with Bitsy.

"I guess I'll have to shoot the persistent devil first thing in the morning. Yes, I guess I will. . . . If I can borrow that derned elephant gun from the cook."

"Now, Charlie." Bitsy patted his arm. "I'll handle him with my frying pan."

Rose Anne was torn between laughter and distress. "Oh, hush up. Both of you." She pressed her hands to her temples. "I have to think."

"Charlie and I will go out there right now and tell him in no uncertain terms to leave."

"No! You can't do that." Rose Anne said.

Both of them stared at her.

"He has as much right to camp here as we do," she added, hoping her turmoil didn't show in her face.

"Well . . ." Bitsy looked uncertain.

"As long as he leaves you alone." Satisfied that he had handled the matter well, Charlie tucked Bitsy's hand through his arm. "Will you join me for a cup of tea, Little Bits?"

Bitsy glowed as if she had swallowed a swarm of fireflies.

"If Rose Anne doesn't need me . . ." She glanced at her niece.

"Scoot, Auntie. I'm exhausted. I think I'll turn in."

Rose Anne hurried inside her tent.

Sid was determined that Rose Anne not be able to ignore him. Although he could have set up camp within six feet of her in the thick darkness without arousing her attention, he made all the noise he possibly could. He clanged the tent poles together and rattled his cooking utensils and banged his gear around.

By the time he had set up camp, he was absolutely certain she knew that he had come to stay.

He stood in a single sliver of moonlight and gazed at the campsite across the way. Rose Anne was silhouetted inside her tent. Even her shadow was beautiful.

He reached for his guitar and caressed the wood like a lover. Music roared through his mind.

Across the way, Rose Anne lay down on her cot.

He slung the guitar around his neck and placed his hands upon the strings. He would pour out his love to her, just as he had in Paris. He would woo her and win her—all over again. But this time it would be for himself.

The first chord vibrated through his fingertips.

Inside her tent Rose Anne jerked upright.

Sid paused, watching her. Slowly she arose from the cot and stood in the center of her tent, facing toward him.

The music clawed at his soul, striving to break free. But Sid held back.

The music touches me in ways I've never been touched, she had told him.

He possessed a powerful weapon. He had used it once, to win her for Luther. And nothing had come of it except heartbreak and pain.

Slowly he unstrapped his guitar and put it aside. Winning her for himself was a lovely dream while it lasted. But the harsh reality was that he had deceived her, and she hated him.

The best he could hope for now was forgiveness. His duplicity had made an unlikely love impossible.

Sid went inside his tent and undressed in the dark.

Rose Anne stood in her tent with her hand over her heart, waiting for the music. Every muscle in her body tensed as she listened, but all she heard was the distant murmur of the river and the chilling call of some far-off animal.

Had her mind played tricks? Had she only imagined the soft strain of guitar music?

She waited in the darkness, torn between praying that it would come and hoping it would not. Her legs and back grew stiff from standing still for so long. She strained her ears.

There were no sounds except the whisper of the wind and the subdued roar of the river.

At last, resigned that the music would never come, Rose Anne climbed back under her covers.

The fashion shoot started the next day. A crew from *Panache* magazine descended on the campsite, turning it into bedlam.

Rose Anne was glad for the activity. It kept her mind off the tall, dark pilot and his passionate music.

The first shots were to be taken near the campsite by the river. Dressed in a brightly colored sarong, Rose Anne sat in the shade of an open tent, having her hair arranged.

Bitsy bustled by, breathless with romance and bristling with anger. "He's standing over yonder like some giant from a fairy tale, just staring at you."

"Who, Auntie?"

"That outrageous navy pilot. You mean you haven't seen him?"

Of course she had seen him. Every nerve in her body was tingling and every bone was turning to butter. But she wasn't about to admit any of those things.

"Just pretend you don't see him, Auntie."

"That's right hard to do. He's about as tall as a

mountain and twice as rugged. Besides that, he looks like he's up to something."

"Maybe he left all his tricks in Paris, along with his wretched buddies."

"We should be so lucky. I think I'll go over there and give him a piece of my mind . . . after I see what Charlie wants."

Charlie Lazarre was motioning to Bitsy from the front of his tent. Bitsy fluffed up her hair and smoothed down her new safari skirt.

"Coming, Charlie," she said in the sweetly seductive voice she had lately adopted for him.

Rose Anne smiled and tried not to look toward Sid Granger's camp.

Let him stand over there. What did she care?

She stole a glance at him from under her eyelashes. It was a mistake. She felt as if she had been punched in the stomach.

"Is anything wrong, Rose Anne?" the hairstylist asked. "Did I pull too hard?"

"No. Nothing's wrong."

Nothing except a TOPGUN pilot who courted for another then flew all the way to Africa to apologize. If she ignored him, maybe he would go away. And then she could go back to being rich and famous . . . and lonely.

Seven

All morning Sid watched her from afar. When the shoot broke for lunch, he sent her a note, asking for an audience. She returned it unopened with a message of her own scrawled across the front of the paper. *Leave.*

Patiently he sent her another, more urgent note. *Please read this,* he wrote on the front of the paper.

She looked up to catch his eye, then tore it to bits with him watching.

Sid turned and walked away.

She might have thought he had gone for good, except that his tent was still standing. After lunch she tried to keep her mind on her work, but all she could do was wonder what was in the notes she hadn't read and what Sid was up to.

That evening she found out. Just as they were all sitting down to dinner, Sid strolled into their mess tent, strumming his guitar. Bitsy and Charlie made a move to rise, but Rose Anne shook her head at them.

"Ignore him," she whispered to Bitsy. "He'll go away."

"Your entertainment is free this evening, folks,"

Sid said, strumming chords as he strolled among the tables. "Compliments of the U.S. Navy."

The crew clapped and yelled. They had no idea why he was there, nor did they stop to question. Theirs was a crazy business, full of crazy people.

Sid began to sing, looking straight at Rose Anne.

"There once was a lady named Ruby/ Who wouldn't say hi-diddly to me/ I sang and I played/ I even stood on my head, but Ruu-by/ She showed me the door."

Rose Anne tried to keep a straight face. Ruby? His pregnant sister, big as a washtub. The song was outrageous and silly, totally unlike anything he had sung in Paris, but it brought back the good times.

Sid's audience laughed and clapped as he threw back his head and began to yodel.

Rose Anne rearranged her food with her fork, all the time trying not to come under his spell. *Damn the man*. Why did he have to be clever and funny as well as talented and devastatingly passionate?

His chorus finished, Sid came back to Rose Anne's table and stood staunchly before her, singing his second verse.

"Oh, Ruby, my heart is done busted/ 'Cause you think I'm a man can't be trusted/ Oh, take back your tears, and lend me your ears/ Just please don't you show me the door."

As he segued into the chorus, he leaned down to whisper. "What's this I see, Ruby? Could it be a smile?"

Rose Anne clamped her lips tightly together, but she could do nothing about the twinkle in her eye.

"The man's outrageous," Bitsy said as Sid strolled through the laughing crowd, yodeling. "Coming here after all he did to you in Paris. I ought to twist that nose of his into a pretzel."

"It's all right, Auntie. Just let him sing."

"You're not going to be crying and losing sleep over him again, are you?"

"After what he and his buddies did to me? No way."

But even as she made her denial, Rose Anne's gaze followed Sid. She knew she had told a lie. Whether Sid was making love or laughter with his music, he was full of a dark fire that burned when she came within his spell.

"Excuse me, Auntie," she said while his back was turned. "I'm going to my tent to read."

"You didn't eat enough for a fly."

"I don't want to look like a dough ball in the swimsuits tomorrow."

Before Bitsy could say anything else, Rose Anne escaped into the darkness.

When he turned to sing the third verse, Sid noticed that she was gone. He unslung his guitar.

"That's all, folks," he said.

The crowd clapped and begged for more. Sid merely smiled and held up his hand as he hurried out of the mess tent.

He found her outside her tent, sitting in a camp chair, holding a novel and staring into space. He was already at her side before she noticed him.

"Hello, Rose Anne."

"Go away, Sid."

He knelt beside her, smiling. "Does this mean you didn't like my song?"

"Acting the court jester again, Sid?"

"It's not an act; it's the real me."

"I thought the real you was the man who seduced women in secret for his friends."

Sid was silent, letting her get her anger out of her system.

"Or was the real you the man who pretended to hate romantic poetry, then stood under my balcony in the dark, courting me with it? Or could it have been the man who betrayed my trust, even when I told him I despised lies and liars."

"All you say is true."

"At least one of us is truthful."

"Everything is out in the open now, Rose Anne. There's no more need for subterfuge."

"There's no more need for anything. The game is over. You can go home now."

"Not until I make you understand that my intentions were good." He reached for her hand, and was relieved when she didn't draw back. "I never meant to hurt you, fair one. Never."

She stared at him with eyes so impossibly bright, he thought he was seeing the sun. He leaned closer, almost blinded by her beauty.

"Oh, please . . ." She put her free hand to her throat. "Don't."

"Don't what?" he whispered.

"Don't seduce me with your eyes."

Sid forgot all the reasons he had come to Africa. "Do I seduce you?"

"Always."

"Rose Anne . . ." He leaned closer, drinking in her nearness, consumed by his love.

His lips brushed hers, as fleeting as the touch of angel wings. It was not enough. With a groan he tangled his hands in her hair, drawing her closer. And she came to him, urgent and hungry.

The wildness in her always took him by surprise. That a woman so perfect, so beautiful, could be such a creature of passion with him was beyond his imagination. It was as if her touch worked a kind of magic, changing him from a toad into a Prince Charming.

In that brief moment while they kissed, Sid believed his love to be possible. He believed in a future so glorious, his heart hurt just to think about it. He believed in a home with room for dogs and children . . . and Rose Anne waiting at the gate. He believed and he longed.

He poured everything he felt for her into his kiss—the tenderness, the desire, the dreams.

And Rose Anne wanted it all. His vision of the future was so bright that she caught a glimpse of it, *felt* it in the kiss.

She struggled against her feelings, struggled to overcome the gentleness, the passion, the visions. Moaning softly, she lifted her hands to shove at his chest, but all she managed was a languorous caress.

Sid's hands moved over her, hot through the thin fabric of her blouse, insistent as they molded the sides of her breasts.

"Don't," she whispered against his lips. She was close to being over the edge. One more intimacy, and there would be no turning back. "Oh, please, don't."

He released her immediately.

"I didn't mean to take advantage of you, Rose Anne."

Shaken, she leaned back in her chair and closed her eyes.

"If you have any honor at all, please go," she whispered.

Sid stood beside her chair, honor battling desire, reason warring against need.

"I'll go . . . for now. But I intend to stay until you talk to me." His dark eyes held hers. "I've laid siege to your camp."

She watched him walk away. He had laid siege to more than her camp: He had laid siege to her heart.

The next day's shoot was at Victoria Falls.

All day Rose Anne went through her paces. To complicate matters, the press arrived in force. In between photography sessions she gave interviews. It was exhausting.

By the end of the day all she wanted was solitude. While the crew and the press packed up their equipment, Rose Anne walked on the perimeters of the makeshift set.

Bitsy caught up with her. "Charlie's got the Jeep ready to go back to camp, honey."

"It's so beautiful here by the falls, I'd like to stay awhile longer."

"Fine. We'll stay as long as you like."

"I don't want to hurt your feelings, Auntie, but I really would like to be alone. Could you and Charlie go ahead, then send the driver back for me in about an hour?"

"Well . . . I don't know."

Rose Anne tucked her arm through Bitsy's and led her toward the Jeep. "It's perfectly safe here, the camp is actually within walking distance, and besides that, you and Charlie could use the time alone."

Bitsy's face glowed. "You think he likes me?"

"I think he's in love with you."

"At my age! I never thought it would happen."

"Scoot, Auntie. And give Charlie an extra big kiss for me."

"How did you know we'd been kissing?"

"It shows all over you."

Rose Anne put Bitsy into the Jeep, then waved as she and Charlie drove way, the last ones to leave.

Dust from the departing Jeeps died away, and there were no sounds except the music of the falls cascading into the river. Blessed solitude. The perfect place to think.

Rose Anne sat on a smooth rock downstream from the falls, tucked her chin onto her knees, and gazed out over the water.

• • •

High above her, Sid kept his watch. He had come early to the outcropping of rock to write and soak up the beauty of the falls . . . and fate had sent him Rose Anne.

When the last Jeep disappeared from sight, he laid aside his notebook. She was alone, would be alone for the next hour if he had overheard correctly. Now would be a perfect time to talk to her. As he watched, she pulled off her shoes and dangled her feet in the water.

Sid was reminded of his boyhood, of all the lazy, innocent summer days when he had slipped down to the creek when he wanted to be alone. There was something about water that encouraged both solitude and thought.

He changed his mind about joining her. She had been surrounded all day long. She needed time to herself.

Moving quietly so he wouldn't attract her attention, he gathered his notebook and his picnic supplies. The walk back to his camp would be long.

Before he left he turned for one last look at her. With her face tipped up to the sun, she slowly peeled away her shirt. It floated to the rock.

Sid couldn't move. Her breasts were high and proud, perfectly formed. She was so fair, so smooth that her skin seemed to swallow the sun. She glowed.

At that moment Sid knew what it meant to covet. When Rose Anne lifted her hair off her neck, arching her breasts toward him, he almost sank to his knees with desire to possess her.

When she unfastened her skirt, he turned his back on her. He had caught her in a private moment, one not meant to be shared. Whether she was merely planning to cool herself in the late afternoon breeze or cavort in the water, he didn't know. All he knew was that he would not invade her privacy by watching.

Quietly he began his descent. The whine of tires caught his attention as a Jeep squealed to a stop just on the other side of Sid's perch. He had been so mesmerized by Rose Anne that he hadn't noticed its approach.

An enterprising reporter, still wearing his press badge, bailed out of the Jeep at a run. Apparently word had gotten around that Rose Anne hadn't returned to camp, and he was determined to have an exclusive interview.

Fifty feet more and the reporter would be around the rock, snapping pictures that would sell in every sleazy tabloid in the country.

Sid flung his pack aside, raced across the rock, and judged the distance down. If he could make the jump without any broken bones, he could intercept the reporter before he got the photograph of his lifetime.

Giving a Tarzan yell, he jumped.

Beside the water, Rose Anne froze. She was not alone.

She pulled her skirt back on, then reached for her blouse.

"What the hell . . ."

The loud voice was male, and very angry. And it was coming from the other side of a huge boulder not very far from her retreat.

"Get out of my way, you big oaf . . ."

Her hands shook as she slid the blouse on. She had almost been caught undressed.

"A thousand pardons, kind sir. Can you tell me the way to the nearest pub?"

She would know that voice anywhere. It was Sid, speaking loud enough to wake the dead. She bit her lip as she tried to fasten her blouse. The buttons kept sliding out of her nervous fingers.

"Pub? Are you an idiot? This is the African bush. . . . Let me pass."

"What's a drink without a drinking buddy?" Sid's laughter was boisterous.

"Who are you, you fool?"

"A drinking fool in a fool's paradise. Come, my good man. Let's find the pub together."

"If you don't get your big hands off me, I'm going to knock you into tomorrow."

As Rose Anne fumbled with her buttons, Sid began to sing, "Tomorrow," Little Orphan Annie's theme song, in a loud, drunken voice. The other man swore.

Rose Anne tucked her blouse into her skirt, then slid her feet into her shoes. Sid continued to sing, loudly and off key.

She had never heard a more beautiful sound.

"Fool. Let go."

"Sing, my good man. Sing! Don't you know the chorus. Here . . . I'll teach you."

The second chorus sounded worse than the first. Rose Anne didn't know how a man with such a magnificent voice could manage to sound like a wounded rhinoceros."

Fully dressed now, she grabbed her hat and dashed toward the sound. When she saw them she had to clutch her sides to keep from laughing out loud.

Sid waltzed in drunken circles, singing at the top of his voice, dragging the poor, hapless reporter with him. The man was at least six inches shorter than Sid and probably fifty pounds lighter. From time to time his feet left the ground as Sid swung him up by the armpits.

"Put me down, you fool."

Sid turned around and came face-to-face with Rose Anne.

"Glad to oblige," he said.

He dropped the reporter, who landed solidly on his rump. Cursing, the man picked up his camera.

"I came to interview the lady."

"Rose Anne?" Sid turned to her, and she shook her head. "The lady says no." Though he made no move toward the reporter, his voice made it perfectly clear that he was more than ready to defend Rose Anne's right to privacy.

The reporter wavered, then decided not to cross him. With a muttered oath he crawled into his Jeep and drove away.

Rose Anne stared at Sid. The drunken sailor had long since vanished, and in his place was a panther with knowing black eyes and a hungry look. She shivered.

The air hummed with the currents that zinged between them. His gaze never left hers.

"Did you see me?" she asked.

"I saw. But I was leaving . . . until the reporter came along."

"Why were you here?"

"For the peace and quiet . . . and for you."

"I don't know whether I should thank you or accuse you."

"Do both if you like." He smiled, and she almost forgave him.

There was a sound in the distance, and they both looked up to see a Jeep coming.

"Charlie. Coming to take me back." Beside her, Sid was as still as a carving. "Would you like a ride?"

"To paradise and back."

His voice was magnificent, his presence overwhelming. She silently prayed that Charlie would hurry.

"This ride goes only to the camp."

"Would it bother you if I rode along?" He leaned close.

She felt as if he had touched her. Her skin caught fire.

Although she said nothing, Sid saw the answer in her eyes. "I need the exercise, fair one. I'll walk back."

Fortunately, Charlie arrived in the nick of time before she burst into flame. She climbed into the Jeep and sat stiffly in her seat as they roared off toward camp.

Somewhere behind her Sid was watching. She could feel his gaze on her neck.

Don't look back, she told herself. But when they had gone a short distance, she couldn't resist. She turned her head and saw him, tall and rugged, with the setting sun at his back. Her breath caught in her throat.

"Did you say something, Rose Anne?" Charlie asked.

"Hurry, that's all. Just hurry."

Sid took his time getting back to camp. He was restless, uncertain. His expedition to Africa had taken an unexpected turn. Here in the wilds, separated from polite society, he was stalking Rose Anne, wooing her, as surely as he had wooed her in Paris.

What would happen if he won her . . . right on the heels of his betrayal? Until she forgave him, there could be nothing between them, nothing except the passion that always sprung up like spring thunderstorms.

More than that, what would happen when they got back to the real world? He was just a homely aviator with a knack for poetry. She was a woman with the world at her feet. It would never work.

He would stay one more day, and after that, if there was no breakthrough, if she had not forgiven him, he would leave.

Sid made a sparse supper, then ate it with his back to Rose Anne's camp. No need to pour salt in his wounds.

After supper he took a paperback novel from his belongings and tried to read. But the book made no sense. It was just words printed on paper.

He left his campsite and walked. Still, the terror and the wonder of his love clawed at his soul. Finally he could no longer contain it.

Later, at camp, he picked up his guitar and began to play.

Rose Anne was bedded down for the night when she heard the music. She squeezed her eyes and clenched her fists.

"Don't," she whispered. "Please don't."

But the music played on. Out of the night it reached for her, wrapped itself around her heart, and squeezed.

She lay in bed, fighting her feelings, but they were not to be denied. An urgency overtook Rose Anne, and she slid from her cot, moaning softly. She dressed quickly.

The night was deep and still, and it swallowed her up instantly.

Her hands trembled when she entered his camp. He was sitting cross-legged beside a dying fire, his head bent over his guitar, his fingers caressing the strings. He was seducing her, making love to her in the dark.

She didn't know whether she made a sound or whether he felt her presence. But it didn't matter. Nothing mattered anymore except the way he looked at her.

"Your music is too beautiful to keep to yourself," she said softly.

"I'll never share my music with anybody . . . except you." He stood up and pulled a camp chair near the embers of his campfire. "Won't you sit down?"

Vividly aware of his eyes upon her, Rose Anne sat down. Sid moved apart, strumming his guitar softly. As always, the music intoxicated her. Folding her hands in her lap, she fought to maintain control.

"I don't want you to misunderstand why I'm here," she said.

He set his guitar aside. "I never presume anything with a beautiful woman."

"Please . . . don't stop playing. The music is soothing after a hard day's work."

"I'm sorry about what happened today." He lifted his guitar and began to strum once more. With her sitting beside him, music poured from him, overflowing his heart and translating into deeply passionate melody.

"I never thanked you."

"No thanks necessary."

"You saved me from an embarrassing situation."

Remembering how she had looked on the rock with her breasts bared to the afternoon sun, he had a hard time clamping down his desire.

"I had my own reputation to protect," he joked, hoping to offset the steam heat rising from both of them. "How would it look if a high-ranking officer of the U.S. Navy couldn't protect a damsel in distress?"

She smiled. "That makes twice you've rescued me."

"Third time will be the charm."

"I don't want you to misunderstand, Sid. I'm thanking you for today, not forgiving you for what happened in Paris."

The guitar slid to the ground as he came to her. Kneeling in front of her chair, he took her hand.

"Rose Anne, there are some things in his life a man will always be proud of and other things he will always regret. What happened in Paris will haunt me forever. In one misguided moment I agreed to help a friend without considering the consequences."

With his kneeling beside her, she felt overwhelmed. His hand felt strong surrounding hers . . . and somehow right. She should never have come to his camp. Wrapped in the deep blanket of night with his music echoing through her mind and his overpowering nearness doing strange and wonderful things to her body, there was no way she could resist him.

"Is that what I am?" she whispered. "A consequence?"

"You are more, ever so much more." His hot hands caressed hers, pressing erotic patterns into her palms. "You are the glow that lights the shadows, the beacon that burns through my soul. Your name is a crystal bell hung in my heart, ringing, ringing as I tremble."

"I won't be seduced by your poetry." With the lie fresh on her lips, she was being seduced, drowning in him, going deeper and deeper until soon she would be completely under.

"I speak truth, not poetry. The song I played tonight was for you. All the songs I've played since you came through the garden gate have been for you."

"Shhh. Don't." She leaned forward and pressed her hand on his lips. "I don't believe you. I *won't* believe you."

"Then believe this." He cupped her face, drawing her down to him.

She tried to resist when his lips touched her, but resistance was physical anguish. In her limited experience, kissing had been nothing more than a meeting of flesh. It had been pleasant and vaguely stimulating, rather like a visit home for the holidays. Not something you'd want to miss, but certainly not something to get all stirred up about.

With Sid, the earth moved. The sweet urgency of the kiss became a hungry demand. Sid groaned, lifting her from the chair so that she stood pressed full-length against him. Sensation exploded in her. She wrapped her arms around him to keep from falling.

His tongue pressed against her mouth, hot and insistent. Rose Anne blossomed for him, flowered open like a rosebud welcoming the first rains of spring.

"I want . . . I need," she murmured against his lips, not understanding what she wanted or needed, merely knowing that if she didn't have it, she would die.

With their lips joined and all heaven's choruses singing through them, Sid lifted her off her feet and carried her into the darkness.

Rose Anne was aware of nothing except the passion that overwhelmed her, the passion and the glory of being in his arms. The past faded into nothingness and reality spun away. There was just the two of them . . . and the beauty that consumed them.

Neither of them could have told how they got to his tent. All they knew was that Rose Anne was spread upon his sleeping bag and he was leaning over her. The fire burning them was so hot, they could do nothing except try to quench it.

She lifted her arms, and he came to her, his face pressed into her hair and his body fitted tightly against her hollows and curves. He kissed her temples, her throat, and she shattered into a million bright pieces. The music of the night that had held her rapt in Paris sang through her, stealing her senses and her will.

She was flying without wings. She was in a clear

and bright place where nothing existed, nothing mattered except to touch and be touched.

"Sid!" She called his name, wild with wanting.

His lips were hot on her skin, seeking, searching, sending her into a wanton frenzy. She wrapped her arms tightly around him, absorbing his weight, her body writhing with the need that clawed at her.

He answered her cry, met her need. His lean, hard hips took up a rhythm as old as time as he pushed aside her blouse. She was braless, and her breasts were offered up to him like nectar to the gods.

"One sweet sip or I die," Sid whispered, taking what she offered, savoring it with his tongue, his lips.

His mouth was hot and wet on her, and she tangled her hands in his hair, dragging him closer. She could feel the strength and the power of him, the fierce passion.

Moving from one breast to the other, he murmured words so poetic, so erotic, she lost all sense of time and place. Even the clothes that separated them couldn't contain the fire. He rocked in the cradle of her hips, perfectly fitted to her body, perfectly attuned to her movements.

She dug her hands into his back, feeling the solid muscle and the fine sheen of sweat that dampened his shirt.

"Rose Anne . . . Rose Anne." He murmured her name as he pushed up her skirt. His hand was large and warm, and she was damp, waiting for him, wanting him.

"Rose Anne," he whispered, his voice filled with adoration and desire.

She was so hot, so hot, and he was there, his fingers sliding inside her. She cried out again and again, drowning in the waves of sweet sensation that swamped her.

"I want you, Rose Anne," he whispered, his eyes fierce as he gazed into her face. "I've wanted you from the moment you came through the courtyard gate in the House of the Angel."

Suddenly it all came back to her—the secrets, the lies, the betrayal. She flung one arm over her forehead, groaning.

"Rose Anne?" He bent down to her, concern etched on his face. "Rose Anne?" he whispered when she didn't respond, his breath warm on her cheek.

She remembered it all. Pain crushed her heart, even while her body still cried out for his touch. Her breasts throbbed and ached. Her loins were on fire. She wanted to be covered by him, consumed by him.

"I . . . hate . . . you," she whispered, gasping for breath, trying desperately to control the rage and the desire that warred in her.

"No, you don't." His voice and his hands were gentle as he rearranged her clothes. "You only *want* to hate me."

"I hate what you did to me in Paris." Tears rolled down her cheeks. "I hate what you're doing to me now."

He cupped her face and tenderly brushed the tears away.

"Don't . . . please. Let the past go, Rose Anne."

"I can't." She gulped for air.

"You came to me, Rose Anne. Doesn't that tell you something? Doesn't that mean that your heart has forgiven me, even while your mind tries to hold on to the anger?"

"All it means is that I'm vulnerable. You've seduced me with your music . . . just the way you did in Paris."

"Forgive me, please. I never meant to hurt you, then or now. I would travel to the ends of the earth wearing sackcloth and ashes if I thought that would win your forgiveness."

"How can I possibly believe anything you say? Am I to believe what you said in Paris or what you're saying in Africa?" Anger began to replace her tears, but she didn't know whom she was more angry with, Sid or herself. She pushed his hands away and sat up. "How am I supposed to tell the truth from lies? How can I know whether this is real or whether it's all part of another elaborate arrangement with your friends."

"This is real, Rose Anne. Believe me."

There was a hungry look in his eyes as he watched her, and she realized exactly what a state she was in. Her hair was disheveled, her buttons were undone, and her face was flushed with anger and passion.

She was at a distinct disadvantage, and it was partly her own doing. Her track record with men was appalling. It was almost as if she had been born with a sign on her back that said "Take advantage of me."

"You're just like the others," she said, "saying whatever is expedient."

She moved apart from him on the sleeping bag and furiously worked at smoothing her clothing.

He studied her with eyes so black, they seemed to have absorbed all the darkness of the night. Even the touch of his eyes set her aflame.

"What others?" he asked.

"Damn you, Sid Granger," she whispered. "Damn you to hell."

"Rose Anne, tell me. What others?"

Her heart slammed against her ribs. The tent tilted, then righted. She thought she was going to suffocate.

"How did they hurt you?" he asked, persistent.

"You want me to name names so you can get

together with them over a couple of beers and gloat?"

"No. I want you to tell me how they hurt you so I can understand your pain."

"I gave them my trust and they betrayed me. Riker Garvin did it the hard way, with another woman in *my* bed. Mike Gordon was a little more subtle. All he did was find out the size of my bank account to see if it would be adequate to cover all his debts."

"All men are not like that, Rose Anne. I'm not like that."

"Go tell it to someone who will believe it."

Sid stood up, a powerhouse of a man who made the tent seem small.

"I'd give the world to undo the last two weeks. But I can't, Rose Anne. I can't take it all back. All I can tell you is that I set out to help a friend . . . that was all. I didn't foresee hurting you." He knelt beside her, his face close, his eyes fierce. "You're the last person in the world I want to hurt."

"I'm an easy target. The Face is always good for a bet among navy buddies or a ticket to easy street. Everybody knows that the rich and the famous have no heart." She stood up, toe to toe with him, determined to look straight into his face if it killed her.

And it just might. In spite of her rage, she still wanted him. She was going to have to join a convent in order to escape from him . . . and from herself.

"Rose Anne, let me—"

"No." She held up her hand, cutting him off. "I don't want you to do anything except get out of my life. The sooner, the better."

She stormed away, then, at the tent opening, spoke over her shoulder.

"Whatever the bet was this time, tell them you lost, Eagle."

His gaze held her for a small eternity, and both of them died a little inside.

"We both lost, Rose Anne."

Eight

Rose Anne awoke before dawn, filled with a strange sense of loss. Exhaustion weighed down her body, and tension pounded through her head. It had been an almost sleepless night.

She closed her eyes and tried to go back to sleep, but something nagged at her mind. Slowly she threw back the covers and went outside. The camp was still buttoned up against the night. The Jeeps stood silent; the tent flaps remained closed. No sound marred the predawn stillness.

Pressing her hands against her throbbing temples, Rose Anne turned to go back inside her tent. Something—a sound, a feeling, a compulsion—caused her to look in the direction of Sid's camp.

She sucked in her breath.

The tent was gone, the camp stool had disappeared; even the signs of the campfire had been wiped out. There was no evidence that Sid had ever been there.

He's moved camp, she thought, but she didn't really believe it.

Ducking inside her tent, she grabbed her shoes and a flashlight and set off toward the river. She must have run the distance, for when she rounded the bend, she was out of breath.

The grasslands seemed to sway in the early morning breeze. As far as Rose Anne could see, the pale grasses moved, tinted pink by the approaching dawn. No silver plane marred the horizon. No tall pilot emerged with the rising sun.

"He's gone," she said.

The river caught her voice and carried it downstream, murmuring in sympathy.

Rose Anne turned back toward camp. She had Bitsy and Charlie. She had her job.

She would throw herself into her work. She would accept every assignment that came her way, no matter how it crowded her schedule. She would live, breathe, and eat modeling until there was no time left to think . . . no time and no energy to remember a man called Eagle.

Sid rejoined his buddies in Paris. He checked into an ordinary hotel as far away from the House of the Angel as he could get. The room had a bed, a closet, a bathroom, and no piano. Even the bar in the hotel didn't have a piano.

He didn't care if he never heard another note of piano music.

Hawk, Gunslinger, and Lightning observed Sid's dark and brooding look and decided to steer clear of any topic relating to Africa. But Panther always stepped in where angels feared to tread.

"Hey, Eagle. How did it go in Africa?"

"I'll tell you when I can pull myself together. My nose left before I did, and I haven't caught up to it yet."

Panther was undaunted. "Did you see the lovely Rose Anne?"

"I saw her, but she saw me first and ran the other way."

"Ask for salacious details and all I get is the runaround." Panther threw up his hands in disgust.

"Catch, Panther." Gunslinger tossed him a beer. "It's good for what ails you?"

"What's that?"

"A thick head. When Eagle starts in on the nose jokes, he's either in a good mood or telling you to mind your own business."

The others agreed with Gunslinger, and steered the conversation to less dangerous waters—where to find the best French pastries and the prettiest French girls.

Every now and then Eagle tuned in so he could throw his buddies off the scent with a pun, but mostly he thought about his dilemma.

He had lost Rose Anne. No matter how he looked at the problem, the bottom line was the same. He had wooed her and won her for Luther, and in the process she was lost forever to him. Pursuing her would only add to her pain . . . and to his.

Life goes on, he thought. But it would never be the same.

Rose Anne had Charlie set such a hectic schedule for her that she barely had time to eat, let alone think. Each night she fell into her bed, too exhausted to know where she was, or even to care.

It was a hard life, but it was the way she survived.

Three weeks after she left Africa, Rose Anne sat on the balcony of her apartment in Atlanta, drinking iced tea with Bitsy and Charlie.

"You don't have to accept this invitation if you don't want to, honey," Bitsy said.

"That's right, Rose Anne. This is not an assignment, just a flattering invitation from Senator Wyland." Charlie took a sip of tea, then reached for a chocolate chip cookie.

He took a bite, then rolled his eyes. "These are delicious, Little Bits. You cook as good as you kiss."

"Charlie!"

Rose Anne laughed. "Don't mind me, you two. Just tell me when the plane leaves for Norfolk."

Bitsy leaned forward in her chair. "Honey, I really don't think you should go. You've been on the road constantly since we left Africa. You're exhausted."

"No, I'm not. I'm just hitting my stride." Rose Anne looked out over the skyline of Atlanta. It was the first time she ever remembered not getting a lift from being home.

"I wish you'd change your mind," Bitsy said. "It's just some old party for political bigwigs. These senators always want to parade celebrities around during election year."

"Now, Bits." Charlie patted her hand. "It's far more than that. This is a very prestigious affair, a change of command at Norfolk, followed by a reception. At least six senators are going from Washington, and there's even talk that the vice president will be there."

"And so will I. My mind is made up." Rose Anne stood up.

Bitsy sighed. "When do we leave, Charlie?"

"I'm going alone, Auntie." Bitsy started to protest, but Rose Anne leaned down and hugged her. "You're wearing yourself to a frazzle, following me around, Auntie. Besides, you and Charlie have tickets to the opera. You're staying right here in Atlanta, and I want to be the first one to hear the good news when I get back."

Charlie cleared his throat and wiped his face with a black dotted silk handkerchief.

"What news?" Bitsy asked, blushing.

Rose Anne smiled. "I believe it all started in Africa when I went to your tent before sunrise the day Sid left and you weren't there, Auntie."

"Well . . . my arthritis was acting up, and I couldn't sleep."

Bitsy glanced at Charlie for support in her lie, and they both burst into laughter. Charlie laughed so hard, he had to wipe away tears.

"It wasn't your arthritis acting up, as I recall, Bits." He patted his lap. "Come here, sweetheart. The cat's out of the bag."

"I'm going shopping, you two," Rose Anne told them, smiling. "Just make yourselves right at home. I'll be gone a *long* time."

A week later, sitting in the plane winging northward, Rose Anne chuckled about what had happened that day. By the time she got back from her shopping trip, Charlie and Bitsy had set a wedding date. She didn't know how long they might have gone on pretending there was nothing between them if she hadn't given romance a little shove.

Rose Anne rummaged in her carry-on bag, looking for the invitation. She was happy for her aunt. Bitsy deserved to find love, even if it had eluded Rose Anne.

As her hand closed around the invitation, she remembered what Sid had said in Paris. *Love. Another silly notion.*

"You were right, Sid," she whispered. "For some it's not only a silly notion, it's a hurting notion."

She pulled the invitation from the envelope to see whose reception she would be attending. She hadn't asked Charlie. Hadn't really cared. These days she functioned quite well as long as she was on the move.

The invitation was embossed on heavy bond paper. And on the front was the insignia of the U.S. Navy.

Rose Anne's heart tried to beat its way out of her chest. She pressed her hand to her throat and took a deep breath.

Norfolk. Why hadn't she remembered that it was a naval air station?

She smoothed her hands over the insignia. How many people were in the navy? Hundreds of thousands? Surely, if there was any kindness in the world, any justice, she wouldn't run into the one man she was trying to avoid.

She opened the invitation and saw the name— Commander Sidfield Cyrus Granger. Not lieutenant commander, but *commander.* Obviously he had received a promotion and the change of command was for him. The reception was for him.

Just looking at his name made her feel faint. She stuffed the invitation into the envelope and stared out the window. There was nothing to see except gray and white cloud banks, stacked on top of each other. Not one single strip of blue sky showed through.

The captain's voice came over the intercom. "We're beginning our descent into Norfolk. We should be at the gate by five o'clock."

Only three hours until the ceremonies started. Maybe she could get a flight back. She'd call the senator from the airport and say she had suddenly taken ill. She *was* ill. Butterflies batted around her stomach. Her heart didn't feel right. Her throat ached. Her head swam.

She pressed her hands to her temples.

"Are you all right, miss," the man seated next to her asked.

"Yes," she said, trying to smile.

Damn you, Sid Granger.

She looked out the window. The plane was out

of the clouds and Norfolk was in view. Somewhere down there, Sid waited for her.

Travelers jumped out of their seats and crowded the aisles the minute the seat belt light blinked off. Rose Anne sat still, staring out the window. She wondered where she would end up if she just stayed on the plane and went wherever it took her.

"After you, miss," her unknown travel companion said.

There was something comforting about strangers. No performance pressure. No need to make small talk.

She got her bag and took her place in the crowded aisle. Sid wouldn't be waiting, of course. Chances were, he didn't even know she was coming.

Still . . . there was no need to play with fire. She'd make her call to the senator from the first pay phone she saw.

"Rose Anne!" a voice called. "There she is. Rose Anne!"

Senator and Mrs. Wayne Wyland were waiting for her in the airport.

Rose Anne lifted her chin, pasted her famous smile in place, and went to meet them.

Mrs. Wyland took her hands. "I can't believe I'm finally getting to meet you."

"I told you the state of Georgia would be represented in style at this bash. What other state can boast having the most beautiful woman in the world?" The senator's booming voice caused heads to turn in their direction. "Welcome, my dear. Thank you for coming."

Rose Anne made all the appropriate remarks. Her heart was finally back in rhythm and her head had stopped swimming.

Facing Sid Granger suddenly became a matter of state pride as well as personal pride. She would go, and if she could get through it, she could get through anything.

The Officers' Club was filled with men in dress whites and women in colorful party attire. From the looks of the crowd, every officer at Norfolk had a woman on his arm—every officer except Sid.

He sipped his champagne and made polite conversation. Everybody wanted to congratulate him. Fellow officers shook his hand and politicians pounded his back.

It was a proud moment for Sid, but he had never been much of a party animal. All in all, he'd rather have been in the sky, racing toward the sun.

Senator Lewis Montfort from Kentucky pumped Sid's hand. "We're proud of you, Commander. Mighty proud. We're counting on you to show the navy what an old Kentucky boy can do with a squadron."

"Yes sir. I intend to."

Someone plucked Sid's sleeve from behind. He turned, and that's when he saw her. The Face. She was standing on the far side of the room, surrounded by a sea of officers.

The impact of seeing her so unexpectedly jolted him into rigid silence. His hand froze on the champagne glass and his mind shut down. Nothing mattered, no one existed, except the beautiful woman across the room.

She was dressed in a simple black gown that bared her lovely throat and shoulders. Her heavy silken hair was pulled back in a snood, and she wore no jewelry.

Unable to move, Sid stared at her. Vaguely he heard the buzz of conversation around him, but he was beyond listening, beyond talking. The face that had haunted his dreams for weeks beckoned him.

"Excuse me," he said as he made his way toward Rose Anne.

The officers surrounding her surged back together, and she disappeared from view. Sid cursed under his breath.

People called out to him as he passed by, and a few tried to detain him, but he moved irrevocably forward. He had one goal, one mission.

The officers parted when they saw him coming, leaving a pathway that led straight to Rose Anne. Her eyes widened and her hands tightened on her champagne stem.

Sid said nothing, but continued his march forward. She lifted her chin and smiled.

One by one the officers fell quiet. A ripple of silence followed Sid's progress. As he came closer, he saw the light that leapt in the center of her eyes, the faint flush that colored her cheeks.

Still, he said nothing. Her smile remained fixed. It didn't touch her eyes.

When they were facing each other, standing so close, her skirt brushed his trouser leg, he spoke.

"Hello, Rose Anne."

"Commander." She inclined her head toward him.

Tension zinged in the air. Passion hung like a thick fog between them. Little by little, the sea of officers drifted away.

"I didn't expect to see you." Sid captured her gaze and held on.

"Nor did I expect to see you."

Her lips trembled ever so slightly. Sid ached from wanting to touch them, to kiss them.

"Would you have come if you had known?" he asked.

"No."

"Then time has changed nothing?"

Rose Anne bought time by sipping her champagne. It might as well have been water. She saw nothing, knew nothing except Sid, standing in front of her so powerful, so passionate, so extraordinarily *male* that she had a hard time keeping her legs from buckling. She had known seeing him would be hard, but she hadn't expected anything like this.

She took a step back, hoping it would help. It didn't.

"Time has changed everything," she said. "You're a commander now, and I'm the busiest model in the world."

"As well as the most beautiful."

He reached for her then, reached out and gently touched her cheek. She didn't blink, didn't breathe, didn't do anything to let him know what he was doing to her.

"If you think you can seduce me again, you're terribly mistaken."

His eyes were very dark, as he caressed her cheek. She hoped he didn't see how she lied.

"I don't plan to seduce you, Rose Anne. But I can never resist touching you . . . even in a crowded room."

His hand moved to her lips. With one finger he traced their curve.

Desire shot through her so hot and bright, she wondered if her skin glowed. His finger moving across her lips was seductive, mesmerizing. Need spiraled through her, and she was almost out of control. She fought to get it back, fought to ignore the heat of his skin against hers, but it was no use. A small sound escaped her.

Sid took her arm and propelled her outside. The balmy Virginia night air did nothing to cool her. She was burning as she always had with Sid, always would with him, burning so hot, she thought she would burst into flames.

He moved swiftly through the darkness, hurrying her along a pathway shaded with trees and sweet with the smell of late summer roses. The sounds of a southern night were all around them—cicadas humming, crickets chirping, tree frogs singing.

They could have been in darkest Africa for all Rose Anne knew. With Sid beside her, touching her, she was totally transported. Reality disappeared. Reason vanished.

When they reached a secluded grove, Sid leaned against the trunk of a massive oak and pulled her into his arms. She pressed her face against his chest, no more able to stop herself than she could stop the sun from rising.

"I told myself I was courting you for Luther," he said. "Even when I followed you to Africa, I told myself that all I wanted was your forgiveness." He kissed her hair, her forehead, her cheek. "I was wrong, Rose Anne. Seeing you now, I know that. All I ever wanted was you, from the first time I saw you."

"You left Africa without a word."

"I thought it was the honorable thing to do. I didn't want to hurt you anymore." He brushed his lips softly against hers. "I don't ever want to hurt you again."

"I wanted you to leave then." She laced her arms around his neck and drew him down to her.

"And now?"

"I don't know." She pressed her forehead against the side of his neck. His crisp uniform prickled her skin and his masculine scent invaded her. "You take away my ability to think. With you, I can do nothing except feel."

"And what do you feel, Rose Anne?" he whispered.

"This," she said, reaching for his lips.

The kiss was a soft joining of flesh that escalated with such speed, it left their heads spinning and their legs weak. With swift, sure movements, he pulled her hips into his. Her chiffon skirts and his navy dress whites couldn't disguise the heat, the arousal. Swollen with need, aching for fulfill- ment, Rose Anne instinctively arched against him, moving to the beat of an ancient inner love song.

Groaning, Sid drew her closer. The buttons of his uniform bit into her tender flesh through her thin gown, but she was beyond knowing, beyond caring.

All the time she was in Paris she had believed it was his music that seduced her, his poetry. Even in Africa it had been the music that had drawn her to his tent.

But now . . . She moaned, swaying in his arms. Now she knew. It was the man she longed for, Commander Sid Granger.

"I can't bear it anymore," she whispered against his lips. "I can't stand this wanting."

He released her immediately. Shaken, she pressed her hands against her chest. Her heart was racing as if she had run five miles. She closed her eyes, inhaling the fragrance of roses and the sweet smells of the summer earth.

"I'm an officer and a gentleman, Rose Anne. I won't touch you again unless you want me to."

Her eyes snapped open. It was what she wanted, wasn't it? That Sid not touch her again? That he not seduce her and make her forget how he had betrayed her, how all the men she had trusted had betrayed her.

"Good," she said, straightening her hair. "I'll hold you to that promise."

Sid studied her so long and so hard that she felt certain he was seeing straight through to her lying soul. She managed to hold still by pretending she was in front of a camera. The right pose for this occasion, she decided, was a look of studied indif- ference. No more confessions for her. No more admissions that he could seduce her with a look, a touch.

Not that she had backed away, not by a long shot. She had practically swooned in his arms. And it had been *she* who had initiated the kiss. Not Sid.

She might think about all that next Tuesday, between assignments in Dallas and Forth Worth. She couldn't bear to think about it now, with him standing so close.

"Shall we go back inside?" Sid finally said, offering his arm.

"Certainly." She slid her hand through his arm, determined not to show how touching him mattered. "You wouldn't want to miss your own party."

"Dammit," he said between gritted teeth.

"Why, Commander Granger, did I hear you utter a byword?"

"In Kentucky we call it cussing."

"In Georgia too, but we would never admit to doing it. At least not in public."

"What's the protocol in Georgia about sharing a drink of champagne with a rejected swan?"

"Are you sure you don't mean swain?"

"With this beak? No, fair one. I mean swan."

She was doing fine until he called her *fair one.* The way he always said it, she could never mistake it for anything except Sid's special term of endearment.

She almost blew her act . . . covering her real feelings with jokes and laughter. Was Sid doing that too? She wasn't about to try to figure out his methods or his motives. All she wanted to do was get through the rest of the evening with as much grace as possible.

"I'll share one drink with you, Commander. We'll call it farewell."

His face was fierce as he led her into the room.

The noise assaulted them. Sid leaned close so she could hear him.

"Call it whatever you like, Rose Anne. But I make no promises."

Sid got two glasses of champagne and led her to a corner, as far away from the noise of the crowd as he could get. Rose Anne was afraid she might assault him in front of two hundred people.

Keep up the act, she told herself. Play it light. She would be leaving tomorrow. Surely she could get through one evening.

"Are we hiding, Commander?"

"Yes. I'm keeping you all to myself for the duration of this farewell toast." He handed her a full glass. Their fingers touched, sending shock waves all the way down to her toes.

"Drink slowly, Rose Anne."

"I'm a disciplined woman. I never get tipsy."

"I'm not referring to your condition; I'm talking about mine. The slower you drink, the longer I'll have you, and the longer I have you, the better I feel."

"You're slipping, Sid. You were more eloquent in Paris when you were courting for Luther." She watched him over the rim of her glass, unable to keep her eyes off him. Thank goodness, her hands were occupied. Otherwise she might have been ripping the buttons from his crisp uniform and trying to take some of the starch out of his body.

"You committed all my love letters to memory. Do you still remember them?"

"They're long forgotten, along with everything else that happened in Paris."

"And Africa? Have you forgotten that too?"

She was certain the hot color in her cheeks gave her away, but she wasn't about to admit anything, especially the truth—that she would always remember the way she had felt in his arms. That she would remember his hot mouth upon her skin until the day she died.

"Africa? Did something happen in Africa?"

Sid's smile was wicked and predatory. "Forgive and forget, they say. Since you've so obviously forgotten, you must also have forgiven."

He was damnably clever. Why hadn't she remembered that? Why had she ever agreed to one glass of champagne?

"Since there is nothing to remember, then there is obviously nothing to forgive," she said.

"I love a clever woman."

"Then I shall spend the rest of the evening being dull."

"I'm amenable. I can love a dull woman too."

She was dangerously close to tossing the champagne glass onto the floor and throwing herself into his arms. The thing about Sid Granger that made him stand apart from other men was that he could make her feel touched without ever lifting a finger.

In desperation Rose Anne tipped up her glass and finished the rest of the champagne in one gulp.

"All done, Commander." She handed him the empty glass. "Good-bye."

When he took the glass, he captured her hand. "What? No pretty farewell speeches? No congratulations? No empty promises that old acquaintances always make to get together sometime?"

"Let go of me."

"I'm not holding you; I'm merely touching you. You're free to go anytime you like." Color flooded her cheeks. What he said was true. "You like it, don't you, Rose Anne? You like my hand upon yours, my touch burning your skin. I see it in your eyes."

"That's champagne you see. It makes my eyes bright."

Still, she couldn't move away.

"Don't keep running, Rose Anne."

Sid Granger could play tender better than any man she had ever known. She dared not think it was more than a clever act, for if she did, she would surely live to regret it.

"Why, Commander Granger. I'm not running anywhere a-tall. I'm just walking across the room to mix and mingle with the rest of the navy." She affected a false drawl, and even batted her eyelashes for good measure. Let him think what he would. Let him think she was a silly fool or a scared rabbit or whatever the hell he wanted to think.

All she wanted was out.

Sid stepped back and bowed deeply from the waist. Then he took her hand and gave it the most lingering, most fervent, most erotic kiss in the history of handkissing. Rose Anne nearly swooned on the spot.

"Until we meet again, fair one." His eyes sparkled. "May it be soon."

"May it be when hell freezes over."

She was so upset, she guessed she flounced when she walked away. So much for getting through the evening with grace.

She marched straight to the long table laid out with every fattening goodie known to man. She wouldn't look back if her life depended on it. Even so, she could feel his eyes on her. The skin at the back of her neck tingled and burned.

Maybe it was a rash. Maybe it was love.

She groaned. Lord in heaven, what was she going to do?

Sid watched from across the room as Rose Anne loaded her plate. He had never seen her eat more than birdsize helpings.

He smiled. She was upset. Good. So was he. Frustrated, to boot. And determined as hell. Now that she had come back into his life, he was never going to let her go.

Second chances were rare. Fate was giving him one, and he was going to take full advantage.

She kept her back staunchly turned to him. Sid moved close to the table and positioned himself so he would be in her line of vision. The brightness in her eyes and the flush on her skin told him he had scored.

He saluted her with his champagne glass, then raised it to his lips.

She held her plate, staring at him, obviously flustered. Then slowly she popped a strawberry between her teeth. Her full lips closed over the juicy flesh.

Sid's fingers tightened on the champagne stem. If she kept that up, he was going to rip her clothes off and have his way with her in front of the U.S. Navy and a few congressmen as well.

She knew exactly what she was doing to him. She lifted one delicate eyebrow. Her eyes sparkled with mischief. And still she kept her lush lips wrapped around that damnable berry.

Sid moved in on her. When he was standing so close he could almost count her eyelashes, he leaned down and whispered in her ear, "Keep that up, Rose Anne, and I'm going to have to fight the entire U.S. Navy to preserve your honor."

She swallowed the berry. Then, lifting her chin defiantly, she popped another in her mouth. If her act with the first one raised his blood pressure, her act with this one almost gave him a heart attack. Looking at him, with her mouth circling the berry, she actually made small humming sounds of pleasure.

Sid clenched his jaw as he watched. When she had finished with the berry, she smiled up at him.

"Do I bother you, Eagle?"

"It would take me all evening to tell what you do to me."

"Why don't you go somewhere, then, and compose another poem or write another song. I'm sure it will come in handy when you and your buddies decide to get up another bet."

"I don't write songs anymore. I left my inspiration in Africa."

Memories stirred in her mind. She clamped down on them. Now was not the time to get sentimental.

"Africa . . . It's a place you lose things, they say."

"I intend to get it all back."

Rose Anne took a big swig of champagne. The thought of being wooed by Sid Granger again left her in need of strong fortification.

Much to her relief, Senator and Mrs. Wyland came by and whisked her away.

Rose Anne wished there were a way she could gracefully leave the reception. But she had come with the senator and his wife. It would be rude of her not to go back with them. Besides, enduring the evening had become a matter of pride.

She glanced across the room at Sid. He caught her eye and smiled. It was a pirate's smile, deliciously rakish and wicked. Rose Anne smiled back.

She had lied to herself. Staying was not a matter of pride; it was a matter of one-upmanship with Sid. The game of cat and mouse they were playing was exhilarating. She hadn't felt this happy since she was sitting at the sidewalk café in Paris, laughing with him over her "pregnancy."

She had never known love could be fun.

That thought drew her up short. Of course she didn't love Sid. How could you love a man you couldn't trust?

He was still watching her. She could tell by the way her skin prickled.

She ate another strawberry, chased with champagne. Sid looked like a tiger guarding a mousehole. Well, she was no mouse. She'd be damned if she'd run.

With a determined smile on her face she turned to the officer standing next to her.

Outside, a rain began to fall. The crowd began to thin out.

Sid and Rose Anne barely noticed. They were still circling each other like two storm fronts, waiting for the clash. The air crackled with the currents that flowed between them.

Rose Anne lost count of the number of berries she ate, the number of finger sandwiches she downed, the amount of champagne she drank. The man who could make her lose her discipline had to be dangerous.

No sooner had she realized that than he was at her side.

"Do you read minds?" she asked.

"Thinking about me, Rose Anne?"

"Not in any heroic context."

"Just being in your thoughts is enough . . . for now." He took her arm. "I'm your escort home for the evening."

"No, you're not. I'm with Senator and Mrs. Wyland."

"They left about an hour ago, or didn't you notice?"

"They left without me?"

"I told them I would see you to your hotel, and naturally, since this whole shindig was in my honor, they didn't want to argue."

"If you think I'm going to make a scene by protesting, you're mistaken. A ride with you will change nothing."

"A ride with *you* will change everything."

Her skin caught fire. Sid Granger the man was as seductive as Sid Granger the musician.

He took her arm, and she allowed it. She even moved in on him as they walked to the car, deliberately promoting body contact.

Without breaking stride he looked down at her, his eyes very bright. But he said nothing. Why didn't he say something? Maybe he couldn't speak for the sexual currents jolting him. She hoped that was the case. If he felt half of what she was feeling, he was probably incapable of speech.

Bolder now that she had survived the walk to the car, Rose Anne scooted as close as she dared to him on the seat, far enough in so she wasn't hugging the door and yet not close enough to seem too obvious. She didn't want him to guess what she was up to.

She hardly knew herself. All she knew was that she was tired of being the pawn in games played by men. Somewhere between Sid's news that the Wylands had left her and his quip about riding with her, she had decided to turn the tables.

The light mist turned to an earnest rain. Sid turned the wipers on, and they made a pleasant swishing sound in the quietness of the car.

He still didn't talk. Neither did she. Her mind was too preoccupied with planning ahead. Did Eagle think he was the only one capable of seduction? He was in for a big surprise—if she could keep herself in control long enough to pull if off.

While they waited for a red light, Sid started whistling softly. It didn't take her long to realize he was whistling the song she'd first heard in Paris. Desire shot its liquid fire through her, and she felt herself going slack. Her legs were turning to butter. If he kept it up, he'd have to carry her into the hotel.

She didn't know whether the whistling was

unconscious or calculated, for she was too busy staring at the rain and pretending not to notice.

The silence became so charged, she was suffocating. Rose Anne scooted an inch closer to Sid and put her hand on his arm. It was a maneuver that had almost caused Luther to wreck the car in Paris. Sid merely smiled.

His uniform was uncommonly bright in the dark car with the street lights shining down. He was darkly appealing in his dress whites.

She pressed her free hand over her hammering heart. "I do hope you're not the kind of man to put me out in the rain and let me fend for myself."

He quirked an eyebrow. "Is that an invitation, Rose Anne?"

"Well, of course not. I'm merely suggesting that you escort me to my room like the officer and the gentleman I know you are."

"What happened to hell freezing over?"

He parked the car and escorted her into the hotel.

"I've always considered people who could never change their minds to be dull."

He chuckled.

"What's so funny?" she asked.

"I was just remembering the first time I saw you in Paris, coming through the garden gate." He punched the elevator button. The doors slid open, and they walked in. "You were so beautiful, you took my breath away."

"I didn't see you. Where were you?"

"Hiding behind the rose trees." He caught her shoulders and turned so they were facing the glass panel on the side of the elevator car. "Look at us. Beauty and the Beast. I didn't think you'd look twice at a man like me. I even thought you might laugh."

Warmth flooded Rose Anne's heart. No man had ever revealed his vulnerability to her.

"There's nothing wrong with the way you look."

"If you overlook the fact that my nose arrives places five minutes before I do." He leaned against the wall, his legs slightly spread, and drew her to him, fitting her hips snugly against his.

Was this love? she wondered. This wild ecstasy that stole her will as surely as it stole her breath?

Sid leaned his chin against her hair. "Even when I followed you to Africa I was still hiding, Rose Anne. I wanted your forgiveness—that was true. But it wasn't the only reason I came."

"You don't have to tell me this." Everything was turning out all wrong. She should be the one seducing, and he should be the one spiraling out of control. She drew a shaky breath and prayed the elevator doors would open and somebody else would get on.

Sid's breath fanned warmly against her cheek, and she felt the hot touch of his lips on her skin.

"I'm laying everything on the line, Rose Anne, because I don't plan to do any more hiding—not behind Luther, not behind false motives, not behind puns, not behind anything."

Her heart was slamming so hard against her ribs, she could barely breathe.

"I love you, Rose Anne," he whispered, his lips against her skin. "If I could turn back the clock, I would be telling you this in a rose-scented courtyard. . . ."

"You did . . . for Luther."

"This time I'm speaking for myself." He chuckled. "I guess an elevator is an appropriate place, after all. Suited to a homely, no-frills-type of guy like me."

How was she to respond to a declaration of love spoken with such tenderness and sincerity, her heart melted? Fortunately, the elevator came to a stop on her floor, and she didn't have to respond.

"This is my floor."

Sid took her arm and strode down the hallway. He walked like a man with a purpose.

Mute, she handed him the key. His hands were swift and sure on the lock. If he felt the same turmoil she did, he hid it well. He was probably used to it . . . having a woman invite him up. A man of his passion. A man with his ability to make women want him.

Don't think about it, she told herself. Don't look back. Seize the moment.

"You still make pretty speeches, Commander." She laced her hands around his neck, determined that this time she would be the one to seduce, then walk away. She expected it to be a liberating experience.

What she didn't expect was his body heat that scorched her through her fragile dress. She shivered.

Carrying out her plan was going to be harder than she had thought. But she couldn't back down, not now, not when she was so close to victory.

"Make love to me, Sid," she whispered.

He caught her face between his hands. "Love is what I will make with you, fair one. Not casual sex. I want you to understand that."

"Then you should understand this . . . I don't intend to fall under your spell again. You can make love to me, and I'll have sex with you."

She almost disintegrated under the long, fierce stare he gave her. Her breathing became ragged. When she thought she might collapse at his feet, begging, he smiled.

"I'll take my chances. I'll make you change your mind."

They came together like two hungry lions. Absence had made the fires of passion burn high and bright. Waiting had honed their appetites. They were ravenous, and a mere kiss wouldn't satisfy.

"Sid . . ." she said with a moan, leaning hard into him. "I need . . . more."

"I know, Rose Anne. I know." He pressed her against the wall, his hands finding the tender swells of her breasts. "So do I, fair one."

His lips skimmed down the side of her throat, as light as the touch of butterfly wings, but hot. Passion climbed high in her until she was moist with it, limp with it.

"You are so beautiful, so very beautiful." He bathed her throat and her cleavage with his warm, wet tongue. "From the moment I first saw you, I've longed for you. Night after night I made love to you at the piano in the dark."

The memories of those nights in Paris seared her mind. How he had made her tremble . . . just as he was now. She fought to hold on to her last shreds of control.

"Do you want the lights?" she whispered, hoping that would show him this was all a game to her.

"Yes. I want to see you . . . all of you."

He moved his mouth over her erect nipple, wetting it through the thin layers of chiffon. She moaned, adrift in sensation."

"You get the lights," she murmured, too weak with pleasure to move.

When Sid left her, she sagged against the wall. He snapped on the bedside lamp, then found a radio station that played dreamy, made-for-loving music.

"I wish it were your music." The confession escaped before she could stop herself.

"I'll make music"—he lifted her and carried her to the bed—"with you," he added as he spread her across the covers.

His heart raced at the sight of her. She was impossibly perfect.

She held up her arms and he came to her. He

contrasted starkly with her, his white uniform against her black dress, his sun-bronzed skin pressed close to her fair, his plain face next to her beautiful one, his big, rugged frame dwarfing her slender body. Only their passion was the same. It enslaved them.

Sid kissed her until his lips felt bruised and puffy. She was pliant under him, her body so slender, it felt fragile; and yet there was strength in the way she moved her hips, strength and a wild wantonness that made him long to rip aside her clothing and bury himself completely in her slick, satin flesh.

She dug her fingernails into his back. "Oh, please, Sid . . . please."

He levered himself off the bed and quickly removed his clothes. Rose Anne's eyes were huge as she watched him.

"You are magnificent," she whispered. "I had no idea a man would be that . . . huge."

He was too far gone for her words to register.

"It's all for you, all because of you." He lay down beside her, bracing himself on an elbow so he could see her face. "I want to undress you, Rose Anne." His free hand traced the neckline of her bodice, dipping downward to tease her nipples. "I want to unveil you slowly, as a goddess deserves. I want to see every inch of your exquisite body."

He played with her nipples until she was moaning softly. "I want to see what I do to you," he whispered.

"You make me crazy . . . mad as a hatter . . . mindless." He skimmed his hand lower, across her belly, and she arched against him.

He felt the warmth of her skin through her silk chiffon dress. Moving his hand back and forth, he caressed her, silk against satin. It was not enough. He had to see her; he had to touch her, all of her.

He unfastened the wide beaded belt that cinched her tiny waist. She arched as he drew it off and tossed it onto a bedside chair. Her soft gown fell away from one shoulder. With one finger Sid pushed it down. Her left breast came into view. Awed by the creamy perfection, the lush ripeness, he stared at her. The nipple peaked and hardened under his watchful gaze. Shivers rippled through her and puckered her skin.

"You do that to me," she said, her eyes wide and bright. "Sometimes, just thinking about you is enough."

Sid felt as if he had been crowned king of some faraway country. Love for her swelled through his heart until he could no longer contain it.

Bending down, he slowly lowered her bodice, his voice rich and musical as poetry spilled from his soul. When she was bare to the waist, he stroked her, mesmerizing her with his magic touch and his golden tongue.

She felt as if she were flying. She arched into his hands.

"Please," she whispered. "Please."

"To know you is to know a perfect thing, heaven come down to earth, full of grace and charm, wrapped in a body so lush that even Venus blushes with envy."

He kissed her shoulder, the hollow of her throat, the gentle swell of her breast. Blindly she reached for his hair, guiding him toward her straining nipple. His mouth closed over it, and she made soft humming sounds of pleasure. He sucked her breasts until she was mindless with passion. She writhed under him, kicking at her restraining skirts.

"A while yet let me suckle here," he murmured, "this divine nectar, fit for princes and kings."

"Touch me . . . oh, please, touch me . . . all over."

He drew her breast deeply into his mouth for one last sweet taste, then slowly stripped away her dress. She had long since tumbled the pins from her hair, and she lay before him, a golden goddess, her long hair spread across the pillows and her body lush and ripe and bare except for a tiny wisp of lace around her hips.

He touched her stomach lightly with one index finger, drawing lazy circles on her silky skin and watching the way her eyes widened with pleasure.

"I will sip here . . ." His finger skimmed lower. "And here . . ." He brushed away the bit of lace until his hand found what he sought. "And here."

She was sweetly swollen, and as she called his name he bent his head to her. White-hot sensations coiled in her loins and rippled outward. Instinctively she tangled her hands in his hair, drawing him closer, guiding him to the core of her pleasure.

What she had felt in Paris had been wonderful, and what she had known in Africa had been exquisite, but who could dream heaven? She glided. She soared. She flew straight into the face of the burning sun and felt its heat consume her. The flames grew hotter and hotter until she was clinching against the heat, crying out Sid's name, over and over. She flung her arms outward and grabbed the sheet, hanging on as the spasms of sensation ripped at her.

Sweat beaded her upper lip and dampened the hair at her temples. When she slumped back, limp and drained, Sid lifted himself on his elbows and gazed down at her flushed face.

"Sid," she whispered, breathless with satisfaction and wonder, her plan no more than a forgotten dream.

Her eyes shone, her lips were softly pouted, and her skin glowed. She was so beautiful, he almost couldn't bear to look. He closed his eyes in reverence.

"Is something wrong?" she whispered.

"No, fair one. Everything is so perfect, I think I must be dreaming."

She raked her fingernails softly across his chest, then slowly downward. Her eyes widened when she wrapped her hands around him. Satin-covered steel.

He groaned. "Touch me, Rose Anne. Touch me."

He covered her hand and guided it up and down his shaft. His eyes blazed at her with an unholy light.

Ripples of sensation started deep inside her once more and grew until she was reaching for him, crying out his name.

He levered himself over her, bracing his hands on either side of her head to hold back his weight. She felt the size of him, hot and hard against her thighs, and she arched to meet him.

"You are so slender," he whispered, "so fragile. I don't want to hurt you."

"You can never hurt me," she said with a gasp. She was frantic now with wanting.

He was gentle with her, entering slowly. She tightened instinctively. Suddenly Sid stiffened.

"Rose Anne?" he said.

She lay still against the sheets, waiting.

Anguish and regret colored Sid's face as he withdrew.

"Don't," she whispered. "Please don't."

"You're a virgin." There was awe in his voice.

"Is that a sin?"

"It's a miracle." He raked his hands through his hair. "Why didn't you tell me?"

"Because it doesn't matter. I'll lose my virginity when and where I please. I don't recall needing to ask anybody's permission."

"You're on the pill?"

She colored. How could she have been so stupid? Of course she wasn't on the pill.

"I assumed you would be . . . ready for this sort of thing," she whispered, worrying her lower lip with her teeth.

"I'm equipped with many things, but not built-in birth control."

She supposed a modern woman would send him down to the nearest all-night drugstore, or, better yet, hop out of bed and go herself. She guessed she wasn't a very modern woman.

Sid bent over her, looking into her eyes, and the silence stretched out until it fairly hummed. He brushed her damp hair back from her face.

"Don't think I don't want you. It's taking every bit of the willpower I possess to keep from plunging into you and taking what I want."

With exquisite care he drew the sheet over her. She clutched it to her chin.

Tenderly he kissed her eyebrows, her cheeks, her lips.

"I'm not prepared to deflower a virgin, Rose Anne."

"I don't care."

"Yes, you do. When you wake up in the morning, you'll be glad we didn't go through with this."

"I think I hate you more than I've ever hated any man in my life."

"That will do for starters . . . good, strong emotion." He loosened her fingers from the sheet and lifted her hand to his mouth. One by one he kissed the tips of her fingers, then he turned her hand over and kissed her palm. There was no tongue, no erotic teasing, just old-fashioned respect.

Her defenses almost toppled. She almost made untimely confessions of love.

Still holding her hand, he gazed deeply into her eyes. "Make no mistake about it, Rose Anne. I will be the one to pierce your maidenhead. But when I do, you will call it lovemaking, not sex. When we come together, it will be because you love me as much as I love you."

He truly was an officer and a gentleman. His wisdom and gallantry made her feel shame.

"Please leave," she whispered.

"I'll go . . . for now. But tomorrow I'll be back."

He kissed her cheek once more, then got off the bed and began to dress. She shut her eyes, praying he would hurry, praying he would get through the door before she made a fool of herself and begged him to stay.

She heard his footsteps as he crossed the room. She dug her fingernails into her palms to keep from calling him back.

In the doorway he paused. "I love you, Rose Anne."

He stood tense, waiting. She remained silent, and the door closed softly behind him.

Nine

The flowers arrived early the next morning. Still puffy-eyed from crying, Rose Anne looked at the card. "I know how you love white roses, fair one. Please accept these with my deepest apologies. I'll pick you up for lunch and we'll talk. Love, Sid."

Love. She was learning to loathe the word. Rose Anne tore the card to pieces, then threw the roses into the garbage can.

"Room service," a voice said through her door.

After the bellboy left, Rose Anne sat beside the window, staring at her breakfast. She didn't even know why she had ordered it. She wasn't hungry.

The perfume of white roses filled her nostrils. Still feeling tearful and droopy, she plucked one out of the garbage can and held it against her cheek.

"Damn you, Sid Granger. Why did you make me fall in love?"

Sid stood at the front desk of Rose Anne's hotel, refusing to believe what he was hearing.

"There must be some mistake. Will you check again?"

"Certainly, Commander Granger." The desk

clerk riffled through his records, looking rattled. The navy provided him with a lot of business. He certainly didn't want to anger a high-ranking officer. "I'm sorry, sir. The lady has checked out."

"Do you know when she left?"

"Early this morning, I believe. Around eight o'clock."

Sid got into his car and drove back to the base. He would find Rose Anne if he had to travel to the ends of the earth—again.

By the time she got to Atlanta, Rose Anne had stopped crying and started thinking. It was funny how you couldn't cry and think at the same time, she mused as she watched the runway come into view. She wondered if you could feel and think at the same time. All she had done lately was feel and react.

It was time to turn over a new leaf . . . if she could just figure out which leaf to turn over. She smiled. Sid had said that in Paris.

Just thinking his name made her want him. It was time to decide why she wanted him and what she was going to do about it.

Bitsy met her at the airport. Her mouth tightened, but she didn't ask any questions until they were in the car going to Rose Anne's apartment.

"Are you going to tell me what's wrong, or am I going to have to guess?"

"I saw Sid Granger."

"Well, I hope you told him a thing or two."

"I did."

"Good."

"I told him to make love to me and even took him to my hotel room, but when he discovered that I'd never been with a man, he wouldn't go through with it."

For once in her life Bitsy was shocked into silence.

"I've got to face everything, Auntie, the truth about myself, the truth about Sid . . . everything."

"Any man with that much self-control can't be all bad."

"Certainly he's not all bad. He's not all good either. I was his pawn in Paris . . . and now he says he loves me, that he always loved me. I don't know what to think or even what to feel anymore. I made two bad choices and I'm terrified of making a third."

Bitsy patted her hand. "We'll take a little vacation, just you and Charlie and me. Down to the Bahamas. Or maybe over at Hilton Head. We've been talking about getting away somewhere quiet so we can plan the wedding."

Rose Anne smiled. "You're a saint. Did I ever tell you that?"

"No. But I think being a sinner is much more fun."

They laughed together.

"You and Charlie are having fun, huh?"

"Fun won't even begin to describe it. I didn't know life could be so delicious."

They left the car and the bags with the well-trained staff, and went upstairs to Rose Anne's apartment. Bitsy went straight to the kitchen.

"I'm going to fix you some hot tea with lemon."

"Please bring some cookies too."

Bitsy paused in the doorway and studied her niece. "Cookies? You're breaking your diet?"

Rose Anne sank to the sofa and kicked off her shoes. "I'm getting out, Auntie. Maybe not permanently. I don't know yet." She raked her hands through her long hair. "All I know is that I've been in this business too long. I think I'm warped."

"You're not warped, honey." Bitsy sat down beside her and patted her hand. "You're just tired."

"Modeling is almost like being in a convent. I've been isolated and insulated. I don't know how to deal with real problems, real people."

"Lord knows I'm not arguing with you, honey. With what you've made you'd never have to work again if you didn't want to. All I'm saying is be very sure of what you want."

"That's what I'm going to find out."

Sid didn't have any trouble locating Rose Anne. All he had to do was call Senator Montfort from Kentucky, who called Senator Wyland from Georgia.

Three days after Rose Anne had left Norfolk, he was in Atlanta. His spirits were high as he maneuvered the rental car through the late afternoon traffic toward her apartment. Flying Tomcats was easier.

When he arrived he straightened his tie, smoothed his hair, and grabbed the flowers. A dozen white roses. He'd picked them up at a florist shop near the airport.

She was not there, the apartment manager told him. Her apartment was listed to be sublet for a year.

A year. Sid was desperate.

"Do you know where she is?"

"I'm sorry, sir. Even if I knew, I'm not allowed to tell you that."

"What about her mail? Didn't she leave a forwarding address?"

"I'm sorry, sir."

Sid found Bitsy Rucker and Charles Lazarre listed in the telephone directory. Bitsy wasn't home, but Charlie finally agreed to meet him.

In the restaurant, waiting, Sid stared across the street at a billboard advertising Rapture perfume—

one hundred twenty-eight square feet of Rose Anne, and every inch gorgeous.

"She's in seclusion," Charlie said as he slid into a chair at Sid's table. "And I'm not going to tell you where she is." He mopped his brow with a purple striped handkerchief. "I wouldn't even be here if I weren't such an old softie."

"I have to find her."

"Why?"

"Because I love her."

Charlie gave that some thought while the waitress poured two cups of coffee. After he had stirred in cream and sugar, he leaned on his elbows and frowned at Sid.

"If you weren't a commander in the U.S. Navy, I would probably doubt your word, but somehow I believe you."

"Then you'll tell me where she is?"

"No. But I'll tell her you came looking."

Sid pulled a napkin from the holder and began to write. When he had finished, he folded it once and handed it to Charlie.

"Will you give her this?"

Rose Anne sat in a swing on the front porch of a white frame farmhouse she was renting in north Georgia. When she first saw Sid's note, written on a paper napkin, she almost cried.

Reading the note, she set the swing in motion while Charlie and Bitsy watched her reaction.

"What does he say?"

"Now, Bits. That's none of our business."

"You better believe it's our business. If he hurts her again, I want you to shoot him, Charlie."

Charlie grinned. "I see that being her uncle is going to be somewhat more difficult than being her manager."

Rose Anne looked up. "He says he loves me and that he'll find me if it takes the rest of his life."

Bitsy studied her niece. "Do you love him?"

"I love his music, his poetry, his passion. I love the way he makes me laugh and the way he makes me feel." The swing idled to a stop, and she shoved off again. "But I don't know if I love *him*, Auntie . . . or even if I can forgive him. There is so much misunderstanding between us."

"Well . . . you can always fly up to Norfolk and find out if you want to."

"He and his squadron have been deployed." Rose Anne refolded the note and tucked it inside her bodice, next to her heart. "He's on a carrier in the Mediterranean."

Sometimes the water was the color of Rose Anne's eyes, so impossibly green, it seemed unreal. Sid stood on the deck of the carrier. The Mediterranean stretched endlessly around him, as if nothing existed except the sea and the ship of sailors it rocked in its bosom.

"Don't jump, Skipper. It would break my heart."

Sid grinned. The only thing that saved his sanity was the fact that Lieutenant Commander Panther Malone was in his squadron.

"It must be bad," Panther said. "You haven't cracked a joke about your shnozzola since we left stateside."

"I'd tell a thousand jokes about my nose if it would win Rose Anne back. Here I am, stuck at sea, and she's God only knows where and I can't do a damned thing about it."

"You've got it bad, Eagle."

"I've got it bad."

Panther looked out over the waters, whistling. He always whistled while he was thinking.

"There *is* something you can do," Panther said, stopping in mid-whistle.

"Why does that look on your face send chills down my spine?"

"'Cause I'm so damned handsome and brilliant besides." Panther winked. "I have all these connections, see . . . and you have all this talent. . . ." He told Sid the plan.

"Even if I consent, she might never know," Sid said.

"Trust me. When I say connections, I'm talking bigtime. She'll know."

Rose Anne was just coming out of the shower when she heard the music. She froze, squeezing the towel until her knuckles were white.

"It can't be," she whispered.

The passionate music she had first heard in Paris washed over her. Dripping water on her wooden floor and not caring, she ran to the radio and turned up the volume.

It was piano music, backed by a full orchestra. Although some of the purity was destroyed by the backup instruments, there was no mistaking the melody. It was Sid's.

Her towel drifted to the floor as she sank to the bed and lay back on the pillows. When she closed her eyes, it was almost as if Sid were in the room with her, seducing her.

A tingling sensation started deep inside her and radiated outward. Her skin began to catch fire. She sucked in her breath as the old familiar feelings took her captive.

Suddenly the music came to a crashing climax. Still tingling, Rose Anne sat up, drew her legs up, and propped her forehead on her knees.

Surely her mind was playing tricks. That couldn't be Sid's music, for he had once told her that he never shared it with anyone. She had been alone too long, dreaming of him.

"That was 'Rose Anne's Melody,'" the radio announcer said.

Rose Anne jerked upright, holding her breath.

"Performed by the inimitable Theo Borgessi," the announcer continued, "and written by the brilliant new composer Sid Granger."

She reached to turn up the radio.

"And now, stay tuned as Borgessi performs another Granger composition, 'Love Dreams of Rose Anne.'"

Sid's music evoked memories of the moonlit courtyard and the fragrance of white roses. She could almost see him standing tall and magnificent underneath her balcony.

Sighing, she lay against the pillows, throbbing with need.

In the middle of the Mediterranean, Sid got his dog-eared copies of slick women's magazines and spread them out. Rose Anne's face stared back at him from every one of the covers.

"Do you hear my music, Rose Anne? Do you know that I love you?"

Week after week Rose Anne kept her radio playing. She didn't want to miss a single one of Sid's songs. When she had to leave the house for errands, she carried a Walkman.

"You've got a radio growing to your body," Bitsy told her on one of her visits. She was sporting a new wedding ring and a new radiance.

"I'm color coordinated. It matches my dress."

"It's good to hear you laugh. You've been doing a lot of that lately. Any reason I should know about?"

"Maybe, Auntie. I'll know in two weeks."

"What happens in two weeks?"

"Sid comes home."

The U.S. Navy carrier quit the Mediterranean and headed stateside. Somewhere in the Atlantic, F14 Tomcats left the deck, one by one, streaking into the skies, lifting so high, they were chasing the glory of the sun, then pointing their slim noses homeward.

In the cockpit Sid chased his own private glory. His triumph at being a part of the burning blue skies was matched by his exhilaration of going home. Six months of Med cruise had made him lean and hungry for all that life had to offer, and he planned to grab it and hold on, starting with Rose Anne. If he could find her.

Rose Anne stood on the flight line, holding her breath as the Tomcat zoomed toward Norfolk naval air station. Beside her, Ensign Herbert Mitchell stood so stiffly upright, he looked like he would break if she touched him.

She shaded her eyes against the sun, watching the powerful silver bird plummet from the skies. It was an awesome sight, and worth every bit of the trouble it had caused her. In order to come on base she had asked permission, produced ID, signed documents. She had done everything except swear on a stack of Bibles and taken a lie detector test.

Jet engines screamed as the Tomcat aimed home, breathing smoke. The plane set down as gently as if it had been landing on a mother's lap, and Commander Sid Granger emerged from the cockpit. Tall and erect in his flight suit, he strode across the tarmac, removing his helmet as he walked.

"That's him, ma'am," Ensign Mitchell said.

"I know."

Even if she hadn't been close enough to see his face, she would have known him by the way he walked. He was a commanding presence, every bit an officer and a leader.

All the breath seemed to leave Rose Anne's body as she waited, waited for him to see her, waited for him to acknowledge her. In spite of the winter chill, she felt hot.

Suddenly Sid saw her. He stopped in mid-stride, his helmet dangling from his hand. He didn't speak, didn't move. Rose Anne's heart almost stopped beating.

Then he smiled and started toward her, powerful, purposeful. She waited for him, hoping.

He halted when he was even with her, not touching, but still smiling as if he might never stop. His eyes glowed in a way that made Rose Anne hot.

"How did you know I'd be home today?" he asked.

"A determined woman can find any man in the U.S. Navy if she knows the right senator to call."

"Are you a determined woman?"

"Yes."

"Determined to do what?"

There was a blur of movement as Ensign Mitchell discreetly faded into the background. Neither of them noticed his going.

Rose Anne touched Sid then. She couldn't bear not to. With her arms laced around his neck and her skirt brushing against his flight suit, she smiled up at him.

"I'm determined not to make a mistake this time," she said. "I've made too many of them already."

"So have I." His gaze captured hers. "Can we start over?"

"You don't know how many months I've waited to hear you say that."

He cupped her chin and tipped her face gently upward. "Did you ever doubt that I would?"

"I've sent you away three times."

"Like a bad penny, I keep coming back."

He moved his hands over her face, as if he couldn't believe she was real.

"I've missed you so," she whispered.

"And I've loved you so, from the first moment I saw you." He traced her lips with his finger. "Don't you know that I can never let you go?"

"I got your note after you left for the Mediterranean, but even then I didn't believe in your love. I didn't believe in it until I heard your music on the radio."

Her lips parted, and he caressed the moist inner lining. She pressed her tongue against the soft pad of his finger, loving the masculine, slightly salty taste of him.

"Your music seduced me all over again," she whispered. Just as you did in Paris . . . and Africa . . . and Norfolk." She drew his finger into her mouth, sucking. "Just as you're doing now."

Sid laughed with pure delight. "Who's seducing whom?"

"I am, and this time for all the right reasons."

"Say it, Rose Anne. I need to hear you say the words."

"I love you, Sid. I've loved your soul since I first heard your music." She laughed from the sheer joy of loving and being loved. "It took me a while to learn to love the rest of you."

"My nose?"

"It's a noble nose. I love it."

"My lips?"

"Hmmm, I don't know about that, Commander Granger. Maybe if I could have a sample, just a little taste . . ."

He drew her close and kissed her to the roar of a very appreciative audience. Pilots descending from Tomcats, officers nearby, swabbies peering around corners—all gave a rousing cheer as their commander claimed the gorgeous woman waiting for him.

Holding Rose Anne close with one hand and his helmet in the other, Commander Sid Granger began the long walk home. The cheering audience came to attention, and Lieutenant Commander Panther Malone snapped a sharp salute.

"Way to go, Eagle," he said, winking.

"They love you," Rose Anne told Sid.

"I love them."

"What does a woman do when she's walking through the base with an important man like you?"

"The same thing a man does when he's seen with the most beautiful woman in the world. Try to act natural."

Rose Anne smiled and waved at their audience. The cheers went up again.

"Did I tell you within the last half minute that I love you?" Sid asked.

"I'm from Georgia. Show me, Commander."

"I thought that was Missouri."

"I'll move to St. Louis tomorrow if that's what it takes."

The laughter that had marked so much of their stormy relationship pealed on the clear wintry air.

"Is there any chance that I can see you in the near future, Miss Rose Anne Jones?"

"How much of me do you want to see?"

"All of you."

She pretended to consider his proposition. Sid leaned close, loving the sparkle in her eyes and the warmth in her face.

"Hell is permanently frozen over, Commander Granger. Your chances are looking mighty good."

"There are some things I'd like to say to you in a properly romantic setting."

"Are there some things you'd like to do?"

"That too." He smiled. "Especially that."

Fate was kind to Sid, and gave him a full moon. It shone through the bank of windows of his second floor condominium, illuminating the grand piano, the large sectional sofa, the candles burning on the low glass-top coffee table, and the bottle of wine.

Sid stood in his kitchen, whistling as he arranged romaine lettuce on two salad plates. Rose Anne would arrive any minute, and he considered himself the luckiest man alive. He had planned to pick her up at her hotel, but she'd insisted on coming to his place.

He added black olives to the lettuce and was reaching for the croutons when he heard music. Somebody was having a party, a very loud party. It sounded as if a brass band were under his window.

Sid paused in his salad making, listening. The music sounded familiar. He came around the bar that separated his kitchen from his den. The music *was* familiar: It was his own, and it was coming from the patio beneath his balcony.

Sid threw open the French doors and leaned over his balcony railing. A three-piece combo was on his patio, playing earnestly but badly.

"What is this?" he said.

Rose Anne stepped from underneath his balcony, and waved the band to a standstill.

"This is a courtship. Don't you like it?"

"I love it. But there's no need for a courtship, fair one. You've already won my heart."

"I didn't win it; you gave it to me."

She wore the same white dress she'd been

wearing when he first saw her. And in spite of the winter weather, she wore no coat. A brisk breeze caught her skirts and the chiffon scarf at her throat.

"You're going to freeze down there," he said.

"I'm counting on you to warm me up."

"I'm ready. Come on up."

"No. First I have to woo you and win you."

"You won me the first time I ever saw your face. Your beauty dazzles and enchants."

"Wait till you hear my poetry."

"Only if you'll let Ensign Mitchell down there hand you his coat." Sid looked the clarinet player straight in the eye. "That is *you*, isn't it, Mitchell?"

"Yes sir." The young man pulled off his coat and draped it over Rose Anne's shoulders. "A few of us like to get together and play when we're off duty, sir."

"Very well. Carry on."

"I hope you're ready for this." Rose Anne had her face lifted upward, and the humor he'd always loved sparkled in her eyes.

"I've been ready for a long, long time."

"I wish I could compose something as lovely as 'Come fall with me beneath this summer sky / And feel the grasses bending with our haste,'" she said, quoting the first two lines of the sonnet Sid had used underneath her balcony in Paris. "Like Luther, my tongue ties at poetry, and I fear I would have composed something horrible, such as, 'Come stumble with me beneath this falling sky / And feel the grasses smushing in our face.'"

Sid roared with laughter. "If you don't come up, I'm coming down."

"Wait." She held up her hand. "Let me finish."

Sid propped his arms on the balcony railing and smiled indulgently as Rose Anne began to quote his sonnet, never missing a word. When she neared the end of the sonnet, she paused.

"What's that?" she said, cupping her ear with one hand.

"Come love me now beneath this parting sky," Luther Snell said as he stepped from beneath the balcony. "And cherish this sweet day before it dies." He bowed deeply, then grinned up at his old friend.

"Lightning! You son of a gun." Sid laughed so hard, his sides hurt.

"You courted me for him," Rose Anne said. "I thought he should return the favor."

"You look good up there, Eagle." Hawk sauntered out from under the balcony, grinning his famous grin. "Like Juliet."

"Oh, Romeo, Romeo," said Panther as he came out grinning. "Wherefore art thou, Eagle?"

"Hark! It's my feet, and Juliet is the nose." Gunslinger came out next.

"Do you have the entire U.S. Navy hiding under my balcony, Rose Anne?"

"I tried, but the rest of them couldn't come."

"Is this where we're supposed to fade discreetly into the woodwork?" Panther asked, grinning.

"Come on, fellows. Let's let this man court in peace." Luther started the exodus, and the others followed suit. When they had gone a short distance, they all turned around and saluted.

"The best man won, Eagle," Luther said. "Just be damned sure you give the rest of us proper credit."

"We couldn't have done it without you," Rose Anne said.

"Do you want to bet?" Sid's eyes gleamed as he stuck one long leg over the balcony.

"Sid, what in the world are you doing?"

"It appears to me you're never coming up, so I thought I'd come down."

Sid found a foothold in the grillwork balcony supports and began his descent. The band struck up an old Elvis tune as they departed with the cheering, whistling pilots.

Rose Anne held her breath as she watched Sid.

"Don't you dare fall and break anything before I get my hands on you."

"Don't worry. I fancy keeping these parts in working condition for a long time to come."

When he neared the ground, he swung down and landed in front her, on his feet, much to her relief.

Rose Anne stood gazing at him, so full of love and wonder, she couldn't speak. "I love you" was easy to say; it was easy to show. But "I forgive you" was much harder to articulate. In the end she had planned the balcony scenario when she had first learned he was coming home as a way of showing Sid that the events of Paris were not only forgiven, they were transformed into a memory she could laugh at . . . and cherish.

And he *knew*. She could see understanding in his sensitive face and his expressive eyes, understanding and love and passion.

He held out his arms and she came to him.

"Thank you, Rose Anne," he whispered, his lips pressed against her temple.

"You're more than welcome."

He tipped her face up with the back of his hand, then captured her lips in a hungry kiss. She shivered from the chill of winter, the passion that assaulted her, and anticipation of things to come.

As his tongue plundered her mouth, Sid cupped her hips and dragged them into his. She clung to him, desperate with a desire that only he could rouse, a need that only he could fill.

In a frenzy of wanting, she arched against him, feeling the size and heat of him.

"Sid . . . Sid," she whispered, moving to the frantic pulsing of her heart.

He lifted his head and gazed down at her, his eyes dark with passion.

"There's some lettuce upstairs that's just about wilted," he said.

"I hope that's the only thing wilted." She arched provocatively against him.

"Why don't we go up and see?"

Sid lifted her into his arms and kissed her all the way up to his apartment, executing maneuvers that she told him would do the marines proud.

"I thought it was a little on the shabby side," he said as he set her on the sofa. "Wait till you see what I do to make the navy proud."

He knelt in front of her. "Do you know how long I've waited for this?"

Leaning down, she cupped his face. "The waiting's over . . . for both of us."

They studied each other, savoring their togetherness. The candlelight picked up the glow on their faces and the shining surface of the glass table and the polished wood of the piano.

"A toast, Rose Anne . . . to love." Sid poured two glasses of wine and handed one to her.

"To love."

His eyes never left hers as they sipped. The Virginia moon was brighter than it had any right to be in wintertime, and it shone through the window, sending its beams over them in quiet benediction.

Rose Anne bent over and set her glass on the coffee table. "I want you, Sid."

"This time for love?" He set his wineglass beside hers.

"This time for love." She brushed her lips down the side of his cheek and across his lips.

Still squatting beside her, Sid lifted her feet onto his knees and removed her shoes. He caressed the bare soles of her feet, sending shivers skittering down her spine.

"One of the things I love most about you is that you don't bother with a bunch of extraneous underthings." He bent down and kissed her toes, one by one.

She made soft humming noises deep in her throat. Sid's hand moved up her leg, scorching her skin. When he reached the moist warm juncture of her thighs, she leaned back on the sofa.

"I never knew that loving someone would make the wanting so intense," she said softly.

Her silky skirts whispered as he slid them upward. "And I never dreamed that you would ever be mine."

He covered her with his hand, loving the way she moaned and the dreamy look that came into her eyes. The wisp of lace around her hips tumbled to the floor and lay in a pool of candlelight. Sid kissed the blue-veined arch of her foot and moved his way up to the softly pulsing skin behind her knee.

She tangled her fingers in his hair and wrapped her long, beautiful legs around him. Her inner thigh was fragrant with the scent of roses, and he feasted there, tasting the silky skin and the sweetness of her perfume.

Memories of Paris washed over him, of how she had looked in the rose garden and how he had made love to her at the piano. Sliding his hand into her tender, waiting warmth, he lifted his head so he could see her face, so he could know that she was real and she was his.

"Do you remember Paris?" he whispered, his voice hoarse with passion.

"I remember how your music made me feel . . . almost like this." His fingers worked their magic, and she began to writhe. "Except this is better."

Her legs tightened around him and she gasped. "This is like . . . flying."

"There's more. Much, much more." He slid his hand upward, pushing aside the chiffon skirt.

She shivered as his fingers drew lacy patterns around the sensitive skin of her stomach. He bent his head and dipped his tongue into the silky indentation of her navel.

The fever of love burned high and bright in her, and she cried out his name.

"I know what you want, fair one," he whispered as he plied her skin with wet, hot kisses lower, ever lower. "I know what you need."

She was swollen with need for him, slick and warm and tasting of musk and honey. With the certain knowledge that this was only the beginning for them, Sid gave her pleasure and release.

When she sagged against the sofa cushions and her legs went slack around him, he lifted her and carried her into the bedroom. The bed was king-size, big enough for a tall, lean man called Eagle and his chosen lady, with room left over for loving. Pools of lamplight illuminated the puffy pillows and the crisp white sheets. White roses stood in a crystal vase beside the bed, perfuming the air with their sweetness. Music played softly, not just any music, but Sid's, the intoxicating melodies Rose Anne had first heard in Paris, taped and coming from some hidden niche in the room.

She knew he had done it all for her. Alone in this otherwise very masculine room, Sid had arranged the white roses and planned the music and spread the clean sheets on the bed in preparation for what they would do there, together, because they loved.

Her heart filled up and she thought she might cry.

"Tears?" he whispered, touching the moisture on her cheek with one finger.

"Yes," she said, knowing he understood, knowing she didn't have to explain or apologize or pretend.

And that was one of the best parts of loving this man.

He set her down, and she slid along the length of his body until her bare feet sank into the plush carpeting. He stood in front of her, his hands barely touching her shoulders, holding her as if she were something precious. The way he looked at her made her toes curl into the thick nap of the rug.

He reached for her hair, took great masses of it in his hands, and watched as it sifted through his fingers.

"The lamplight makes your hair look gold, like wheat in the sun." He leaned down and pressed his face into her hair. "I could drown here."

She leaned into him until their bodies were touching. "Do you feel the currents, Sid, as if you've plugged into an electrical socket? Is it like that for you?"

"Touching you is like plugging into an electrical storm." He wrapped his arms around her, and they held each other, not saying anything for a while, just feeling, *feeling*, and knowing what they each felt was reciprocated.

He was hard against her, and she knew that in him lay all the mystery and the wonder she craved. She brushed her lips against his skin, just inside the open collar of his shirt. Her tongue flicked out to taste.

"I want this to be good for you," he said. "Slow and easy, the first time."

Her tongue made a wet circle on his throat, just where the blood pulsed softly. Sid groaned.

"You're playing with fire, Rose Anne."

She leaned back in his arms and smiled up at him. "Burn me."

His eyes were bright as he undressed her. Slowly he peeled away the soft chiffon dress, starting at her shoulders. His fingers left trails of fire as her gown slid to the floor.

When she stood naked before him, he drew a deep, shaky breath, as if he couldn't believe what he saw. His eyes raked her, starting at her face, moving slowly down to her toes, then back up again.

"The way you look at me makes me feel special."

"You *are* special." He came to her and cupped her breasts. His thumbs teased her already-taut nipples into hard, straining diamond points. "You are so beautiful that every time I see you, it's like the first time, all over again." He bent to her breasts, sucking one while his hand massaged the other.

She arched toward him, giving his mouth better access. Tangling her hands in his hair, she held him close, murmuring incoherent words of encouragement and love.

The dark fire that he could always awaken in her flamed to life, and she knew that this was love. The feeling was new and wondrous to her, and she knew she had never felt it with another man, would *never* feel it with another man.

"Will you always do that, Sid?"

"What, fair one?" He lifted her head so he could see her beloved face.

"Make me feel this small death, as if I've left everything behind except passion?"

"Always, Rose Anne. As long as you want me to."

He captured her lips then, and carried her to the fresh sheets. They were crisp behind her back, and their clean scent washed over her.

Sid watched her as she lay there, waiting for him.

"I never dreamed this would happen." He removed his clothes and lay down beside her, pulling her into his arms. He traced a tender trail from the top of her shoulder down to her wrist, then, turning it over, he licked the tiny network of blue veins that ran all the way up to her elbow.

Her body wept for him, and she cried out, pushing her hips against his. He guided her hand, and she closed it around him.

"You do this to me, Rose Anne . . . and more, so much more."

He was unexpectedly hot, burning steel covered with velvet. His tongue flicked into her ear, and he murmured words that made her bold. Her palm tingled with the knowledge of him. He guided her hand until the tip of his shaft was buried just inside, where she was so hot for him, so slick and wet and desperate that she thought she was going to die. His velvety skin kissed hers, over and over until she was begging.

"You are so sweet . . . so sweet . . ." He eased farther inside her, sending flames licking along her thighs. "And so very ready."

He turned her over so that her hair was spread across the pillow. The swift movement separated her from him, and it was agony.

He braced his hand on either side of her slim shoulders. "I don't want to hurt you, Rose Anne."

Quickened as she was, dying inside for lack of him, she thrust upward, seeking the hot, hard rapture of him, longing for the sweet oblivion she instinctively knew would be hers.

"Now . . . please, Sid . . . now."

He cupped her hips and eased between her legs. In one powerful smooth movement he was inside her, where he belonged. He held still, watching her face, looking for signs that he had hurt her.

She smiled and wrapped her arms around his neck.

"Heaven is worth the pain," she whispered.

Music pulsed around them, and he began to

move. The passion that had gathered in his soul from the moment he saw her came pouring forth. She was heaven . . . and more. He soared with her, learning her mysteries and her rhythms.

For all her virginity, she was a natural wanton, writhing and crying out her pleasure. Tension corded the muscles in his arms and his back as he tried to restrain himself, but Rose Anne would have none of it.

Her slender hips thrust boldly against him, inviting a frantic rhythm.

"I want more . . . more," she whispered fiercely. Sweat dampened the edges of her hair and glowed on her brow. Passion burned in the depths of her eyes. "More, Sid . . . please."

He increased his rhythm, and she raced with him, her nails biting into his back. He rode hard, carrying them both to that high, bright summit that swept away reason. Nothing existed for them except the rapture of discovery and the ecstasy of their passion. Release shattered them at the same time, and they clung to each other, shaken.

When the tremors passed, when he folded her in his arms and drew up against his chest, fitting the curves of her back and hips against him just so, she sighed.

"Are you all right, Rose Anne?"

She reached for his hand and brought it to her lips. "I didn't know there would be this . . . full-ness, this sense of having bloomed, of having ripened." She kissed his fingertips one by one.

"That's the difference between loving and sex. Sex makes you less and loving makes you more."

"I'm glad it was you who taught me, Sid."

"Are you hungry? I think there are some wilted salads in the kitchen."

"Can I wait?"

"As long as you like."

She snuggled closer. "I want to luxuriate awhile."

"Take your time, fair one. When you get hungry, just tell me so."

They lay fitted together, and contentment swirled around them like summer wind. After a while she spoke.

"Sid?" The small, twisting movement she made in order to see his face sent fires racing along his veins.

"Hmm?" He backed his hips slightly away, for her protection as well as his. She needed time for all the newness to soak in, to wear off.

"I don't know a lot about these things . . . I mean about how often a man can . . . hmmm . . ."

"Perform?"

She chuckled. "I was just thinking . . . if it's not too much trouble, I'd like to try it again before I eat."

Laughing with pure uninhibited joy, he rolled onto his back, taking her with him. Still smiling, he lifted her up and positioned her over his arousal. Her eyes widened.

"Do you like that?" he asked.

"Hmmm . . . yes." She rocked with the pure pleasure of it all.

He clasped her hands, lacing her fingers through his in order to give her something to hang on to.

"Carry me on that long, hard, sweet ride to ecstasy, Rose Anne."

She did. And it was a very long time before they got around to their wilted salads.

Rose Anne discovered what it was like to sleep all night in the arms of a man and wake up the next morning, still cuddled close, with his beard stubble prickling the skin on her bare shoulder. She felt exhilarated and carefree and happy.

Their covers were wrinkled and pulled loose

from the corners of the mattress, and one of the pillows was on the floor. Who needed a pillow when she had Sid?

She eased back, careful not to wake him, so she could study him. His rugged face lost some of its fierceness in sleep. Up close his lean and powerful body looked like a work of art. She could spend the rest of her life studying him. And she planned to.

Smiling, she burrowed close to him and wrapped his long arms around her waist. She wondered if today would be the day he'd ask her to marry him.

Burying her face in the curve between his throat and his shoulder, she began to nibble at his skin.

"Rose Anne?"

She loved the way his voice sounded, just coming awake. Even then it was so compelling, it sent shivers down her spine.

"Are you awake?" she whispered, running her hand down the length of his body.

He gasped. "I'm more than awake, Rose Anne. I'm filled with love for you."

"I'm from Georgia. Show me."

Laughing, he tumbled her out from the covers and began a slow, sweet exploration of her body that lasted well into the morning. Afterward they put on robes. He lent her one of his. It came to her ankles, and she had to roll the sleeves four times.

They were ravenous by the time they got to the kitchen. Neither of them was a good cook, but together they managed to make a decent omelet. They laughed at their ineptness. She bragged that she was an expert at opening cans, and he countered by saying he could open any jar lid in the world.

He filled a hot tub for her while she loaded the dishwasher.

Later, in the tub, she leaned her head against

the cool porcelain and smiled. She couldn't seem to stop smiling.

In the bedroom Sid changed the sheets, glancing every now and then through the half-open door at Rose Anne. She was up to her neck in bubbles, and her face was rosy from the moist steam heat of her bath and her recent awakening as a woman.

He glanced at the telltale stains on the sheets. He had touched her where no man ever had. In the deep, sweet darkness of the night she had given herself completely to him, and implicit in the act had been her trust.

Standing with the sheet in his hand, he trembled with awe. How could it be possible for one man to have the whole world while so many had nothing?

"How did I ever get so lucky?"

"Did you say something, Sid?" Rose Anne called through the door.

"Just talking to myself."

"If you're that desperate for company, come in here and talk to me."

Sid crossed the room and leaned against the door frame. She lifted a handful of bubbles and blew them his way. They floated, iridescent, to the tile floor and burst in small soapy patches.

"You told me you wanted a long, hot soak in the tub," he said.

"That's true."

"Then it's best that I stay on this side of the door."

They gazed at each other, striking sparks. Very slowly Rose Anne lifted a soapy arm from the water and beckoned him with one little finger.

He knelt beside the tub. She leaned over and rubbed her wet nose against his cheek.

"How are you at back scrubs?"

"Why don't I show you?"

Ten

They had a perfect lovers' weekend, venturing out of the apartment only when hunger drove them. Rose Anne was blissfully happy, but she waited and waited for the question that didn't come.

"My flight leaves tomorrow." She was standing at the window, looking out into the night, determined to be sophisticated. People in love had affairs. It was the smart, sensible thing to do, especially if one of them didn't want to get married.

"I know." Restless, Sid prowled around the room.

"It's a good assignment . . . in Atlanta, so I won't have to leave home."

"You're back into modeling, then?"

"It's time to go back."

"Permanently?"

"I don't know."

The ease they had enjoyed all weekend left them. They stared at each other, hungry and anxious.

"I can come down to see you next weekend," he said.

She turned to face him. "Or I can come here."

A vision of how it would be loomed in Sid's mind. Stolen, hurried weekends, squeezed between his schedule and hers. Love on the run.

He wanted more. He wanted all of her, all the time. He was like the little boy who had been given the stars and had insisted on having the sun and the moon too. Once he had it all, the sky was left empty, and there was no more heaven.

His eyes searched hers, then he turned and walked to the piano.

Rose Anne didn't know what to do, what to say.

She watched him run his hands over the keys. Music did more than soothe the savage beast. For Sid it was a way of communicating when his heart was too full for him to say the words. It was his way of purging the darkness that was much a part of him. She knew that about him. She understood his complexity.

Music rippled through her as he caressed the keys. She felt each note vibrating along her nerve endings. The song he played was new, a dreamy, haunting melody that brought moisture to her eyes. She leaned against the window frame and watched through her tears.

Sid brooded over the keyboard, pouring out his soul.

As always, the music worked its magic. Need spiraled through Rose Anne. She moved toward the piano, determined that this time there would be no sad good-byes for them. They'd had far too many sad good-byes.

She leaned against the polished wood, facing him. "Is the song for me?"

"All my songs are for you . . . always."

"And all my love is for you . . . always."

She slipped off her shoe and slid her bare foot onto his lap. He sucked in a sharp breath, then lifted his eyes to hers. Her foot moved with erotic intent while she smiled at him.

He played on, never taking his eyes off her. The power and intensity of his music vibrated through the piano and through her hip, leaning so casually against the polished wood.

Slowly she began to unbutton her blouse. As it drifted to the floor, she cupped her breasts and arched her torso.

She was lush and ripe, and her sensuality took Sid's breath away. The music slowed . . . hesitated . . . then picked up again.

Rose Anne leaned toward him and languidly popped her index finger deep in her mouth. She made small murmuring sounds of pleasure as her foot slid up and down his inner thigh.

"Do you want me, Sid?" she whispered.

The song came to a crashing climax as he pulled her into his arms and bent her backward over the keyboard.

"Do I want you?" he said, his voice harsh and his breath warm against her skin. "Does the earth want the sun?"

His mouth was hot on her, and he sucked her greedily, without apology and without the grace that had always marked their loving. She felt the sensations rolling through her, rolling with the force of tidal waves. She rocked and moaned with them, moaned until Sid lifted her up, shifted her around, and she felt the hard, shiny surface of the piano at her back.

He pushed her skirt up and exploded into her, the frenzy and wildness showing in his eyes as the smell of lemon drifted upward from the polished wood. She rode his wildness, welcomed it, reveled in it. He touched the primitive in her, and she sank her nails into his back, holding on, holding on and crying out her need in hoarse sounds she hardly recognized as her own.

She felt the tension building in him, and her own body felt like a storm cloud too heavy to sustain its burden. It seemed to her that her old self had separated from the woman spread upon the piano. From some far and distant place she heard herself asking for more, even as her body begged for release.

Merciless, driven, Sid plowed into her, so hot that his face was shiny and wet. The winds of premonition blew cold across her heart, and she tasted the moisture of his sweat and her tears.

"Don't ever stop," she begged, knowing he had to, knowing that obsession such as theirs would destroy if it weren't tamed.

When the spasms overtook her, Sid planted his seed deep, then collapsed over her, his breath rushing out like an engine run out of steam. She clutched her to him, afraid to let go.

"I love you so much, it scares the hell out of me." His voice was muffled against her throat.

"I know," she said, smoothing his damp hair. "I know."

They lay on the piano, their slick bodies joined, until thirst finally tore them apart. Sid levered himself up, then tenderly lifted her off the piano.

They were quiet as they rearranged their clothes. She smoothed down her skirt, then picked her blouse off the floor. One shoe was beside the piano bench and the other under the piano. She didn't bother with them, but padded barefoot to the kitchen and poured herself a cool drink of water.

Sid came in behind her. She didn't turn, for she could hardly bear to look at him knowing she would soon be leaving with so many things left unsaid. His arms circled her from behind and she leaned against him. They rocked, holding on to each other, still silent.

The ice maker dumped a fresh load of ice cubes. As if that were a signal, Sid released Rose Anne, then went to the refrigerator.

She turned to watch him. There were red marks on his back where her nails had scored the skin. She touched the marks, then kissed them, feeling the tremors that went through him.

"Let me get something for these," she murmured, her lips still warm against his back.

"They'll be all right."

"No. I want to do this."

She held herself very proud as she left the kitchen, and Sid watched her go. His hands tightened on the glass until his knuckles were white.

"Dammit," he whispered, his jaw clenched so tight, he thought he might break his back teeth. How much could he ask of this beautiful woman? How much would she be willing to sacrifice?

Rose Anne was smiling when she came back with the antibiotic salve. To a casual observer it might have looked like the smile of a happy woman, but Sid had seen her happy. He knew the sparkle that came into her eyes, the glow that came into her cheeks. She was still flushed from their lovemaking, and she had the pouty, languid look of a satisfied woman, but she didn't look happy.

"Rose Anne . . ." He lifted her hand and kissed the knuckles. "Is anything wrong?"

"No . . ." She held up the tube of salve. "Turn around, please."

Her hands soothed his back.

"That feels good."

"Hmmm," she said, still working on the marks long after he knew the job was finished. "There," she said, and walked to the other side of the kitchen, almost as if she couldn't bear to touch him anymore.

He hated the constraint between them. "Why don't we get dressed, then go somewhere for a nice, quiet dinner?" he said.

At the restaurant they both tried too hard to be

happy. He began to make jokes about his nose, and she laughed even when they weren't funny. After dessert, which she nibbled and he devoured, she excused herself. In the powder room she leaned against the marble vanity and stared at herself in the mirror. Her eyes were too bright. She wondered if Sid knew how close she was to tears.

Angrily, she pulled her compact out of her purse and dabbed at her cheeks. Maybe he didn't love her enough. Maybe he had never meant for them to have more than an affair.

If that's the way he wanted it, she could handle it. She'd do anything, as long as it meant having Sid in her life.

Anyway, she was being unreasonable, thinking about marriage after only one weekend with him. These things took time. Didn't they?

They lingered over dinner, something they had never done. Always, they had been too eager to get back to his apartment and explore each other to dally over food.

"Ready?" he asked when she got back to the table.

"Yes."

They didn't talk much going back to his apartment, and then only about inconsequential things. He never mentioned her career, and she never mentioned commitment. She didn't talk about the possibility of a long separation, and he didn't talk about the agony of living in separate states.

They were still subdued when they climbed into bed. He held her softly in the circle of his arms, and she lay, wide-eyed, staring at a spot of light through the crack in the blinds.

When Sid's breathing became even, she climbed out of bed and went into the kitchen. She prowled around, not really thirsty, but looking for something to drink, something to keep her mind off the following day.

She poured a glass of orange juice and sat on a barstool, staring at it.

"Rose Anne?" Sid sat on a barstool beside her. "What's wrong?"

"I couldn't sleep."

"Neither could I." He took a sip of her orange juice, then set the glass back on the bar. "Too much excitement this weekend, I guess," he said, trying for a grin and failing.

"I guess."

What was happening to them? They sounded like people who hardly knew each other, making polite conversation.

"I hate this," she said suddenly, surprising both of them. She swiveled on the barstool to face him. "And if you dare say 'Hate what?' I'm going to scream."

He put a hand on her cheek.

"I hate it too, Rose Anne. I hate that you're leaving tomorrow, and I hate being afraid that I'll somehow lose you to your glamorous career. . . ."

"Lose me!" She leaned so close, her nose touched his. "Sid Granger, how dare you think I'm that frivolous. How dare you think I flew all the way up here for a weekend tumble in your bed."

"I don't think that—"

"Yes, you do, and I plain and simply won't have it." She jumped off the barstool and began to pace. "After all the trouble I went to—calling all over the country to locate Hawk and Lightning and Gunslinger, getting my hands on a tape of your music and then finding that combo to learn it, standing out in the thirty-degree weather without a coat just so you would be reminded of the first time you saw me in Paris—"

She paused for breath, flinging her arms out

and her head back as she beseeched the ceiling. Sid strode toward her and smothered her in his arms.

"You forgot the piano," he said.

She pressed her face into the crisp, curly hairs on his chest.

"I did *not* forget the piano," she said, her voice muffled. "I just didn't think 'a tumble on your piano' sounded right."

"Don't you know, fair one, that I'd give anything in the world if you would stay . . ."

"I thought I had finally learned to be a modern woman, but I guess I was wrong. I can't picture myself spending the next few years of my life flying to Norfolk or Miramar or wherever you happen to be for a weekend in your bed."

He tipped her face up with the back of his hand. "Is that what you thought I wanted?"

"Yes . . . isn't it?"

"I want you to marry me, Rose Anne. I want to stand in front of an altar with you and pledge my love to you before God and the whole world. I want you to carry my name and bear my children." His hands caressed her cheeks. "I love you, and love means commitment."

Her smile was radiant. "Why didn't you say so?"

"You said you were going back to your career, and I assumed that you wouldn't be interested in marriage, at least not yet."

"Sid Granger, don't you ever assume anything else about me as long as you live." She traced his lips with the tips of her fingers. "Except that I love you. You can always assume that."

"Does that mean you'd say yes if I asked you to marry me?"

"Does that mean you're asking?"

Sid dropped to his knees and folded back the sleeve of his robe that she was wearing. "If I can find your hand."

"Let me help you." She pushed the sleeve up to her elbow and placed her hand in his.

"First of all, assume that we're surrounded by candlelight and music, that there's a bottle of wine chilling on ice."

"I hear the music."

"Then assume that there's a velvet box in my hand, and inside is the finest diamond you ever saw."

"The sparkle hurts my eyes." She smiled down at him. "Sid, while I'm at it, can I assume a balcony in Paris with white roses growing up the wrought iron trellis?"

"By all means."

"I smell the roses."

"Rose Anne, you are my heart, my soul, my very life. You are the music that sings through my veins and the passion that heats my blood. Will you do me the great honor of becoming my wife?"

She knelt beside him and took his face between her hands. "I will."

They sealed their promise with a kiss as tender as first love. Finally they broke apart, still facing each other, kneeling. By tacit agreement they knew there were still things they had to say.

"I've been thinking of cutting back on my modeling assignments," she said. "Taking only those that really interest me."

"And I've been thinking of early retirement, twenty years instead of thirty. There's a lot of music I'd like to write." He kissed her hand. "Being a military wife won't be easy."

"Being a husband to the Face won't be any picnic."

"I can handle it . . . as long as nobody asks me to put my face on a billboard."

"There *is* someplace I'd like you to put your face, Sid."

"Where, fair one?"

"On the pillow . . . next to mine."

He carried her into the bedroom and laid her gently upon the sheets, an angel who had tumbled from heaven into his bed. Then he lay down beside her and gathered her into his arms.

"I'm on the pillow next to yours," he said.

"Good. That's where you belong."

"Rose Anne . . . did you say I have to be sleeping?"

"Actually, I'd prefer if you didn't sleep for a while."

"I think I'll make a little night music."

He kissed his betrothed on her beautiful face, and they both felt the dark music that stirred their hearts, the dark fire that flamed in their souls. And they knew that neither the music nor the fire would ever leave them.

THE EDITOR'S CORNER

What could be more romantic than Valentine's Day and six LOVESWEPT romances all in one glorious month! Celebrate this special time of the year by cuddling up with the wonderful books coming your way soon.

The first of our reading treasures is **ANGELS SINGING** by Joan Elliott Pickart, LOVESWEPT #594. Drew Sloan's first impression of Memory Lawson isn't the best, considering she's pointing a shotgun at him and accusing him of trespassing on her mountain. But the heat that flashes between them convinces him to stay and storm the walls around her heart . . . until she believes that she's just the kind of warm, loving woman he's been looking for. Joan comes through once more with a winning romance!

We have a real treat in store for fans of Kay Hooper. After a short hiatus for work on **THE DELANEY CHRISTMAS CAROL** and other books, Kay returns with **THE TOUCH OF MAX,** LOVESWEPT #595, the *fiftieth* book in her illustrious career! If you were a fan of Kay's popular "Hagan Strikes Again" and "Once Upon a Time" series, you'll be happy to know that **THE TOUCH OF MAX** is the first of four "Men of Mysteries Past" books, all of which center around Max Bannister's priceless gem collection, which the police are using as bait to catch a notorious thief. But when innocent Dinah Layton gets tangled in the trap, it'll take that special touch of Max to set her free . . . and capture her heart. A sheer delight—and it'll have you breathlessly waiting for more. Welcome back, Kay!

In Charlotte Hughes's latest novel, Crescent City's new soccer coach is **THE INCREDIBLE HUNK,** LOVE-SWEPT #596. Utterly male, gorgeously virile, Jason Profitt has the magic touch with kids. What more perfect guy could there be for a redhead with five children to raise! But Maggie Farnsworth is sure that once he's seen her chaotic life, he'll run for the hills. Jason has another plan of action in mind, though—to make a home in her loving arms. Charlotte skillfully blends humor and passion in this page-turner of a book.

Appropriately enough, Marcia Evanick's contribution to the month, **OVER THE RAINBOW,** LOVESWEPT #597, is set in a small town called Oz, where neither Hillary Walker nor Mitch Ferguson suspects his kids of matchmaking when he's forced to meet the lovely speech teacher. The plan works so well the kids are sure they'll get a mom for Christmas. But Hillary has learned never to trust her heart again, and only Mitch's passion-ate persuasion can change her mind. You can count on Marcia to deliver a fun-filled romance.

A globetrotter in buckskins and a beard, Nick Leclerc has never considered himself **THE FOREVER MAN,** LOVESWEPT #598, by Joan J. Domning. Yet when he appears in Carla Hudson's salon for a haircut and a shave, her touch sets his body on fire and fills him with unquenchable longing. The sexy filmmaker has leased Carla's ranch to uncover an ancient secret, but instead he finds newly awakened dreams of hearth and home. Joan will capture your heart with this wonderful love story.

Erica Spindler finishes this dazzling month with **TEMPT-ING CHANCE,** LOVESWEPT #599. Shy Beth Waters doesn't think she has what it takes to light the sensual spark in gorgeous Chance Michaels. But the outrageous results of her throwing away a chain letter finally convince her that she's woman enough to tempt Chance—and that he's more than eager to be caught in her embrace. Humorous, yet seething with emotion and desire, **TEMPTING CHANCE** is one tempting morsel from talented Erica.

Look for four spectacular novels on sale now from FANFARE. Award-winning Iris Johansen confirms her place as a major star with **THE TIGER PRINCE,** a magnificent new historical romance that sweeps from exotic realms to the Scottish highlands. In a locked room of shadows and sandalwood, Jane Barnaby meets adventurer Ruel McClaren and is instantly transformed from a hard-headed businesswoman to the slave of a passion she knows she must resist.

Suzanne Robinson first introduced us to Blade in **LADY GALLANT,** and now in the new thrilling historical romance **LADY DEFIANT,** Blade returns as a bold, dashing hero. One of Queen Elizabeth's most dangerous spies, he must romance a beauty named Oriel who holds a clue that could change history. Desire builds and sparks fly as these two unwillingly join forces to thwart a deadly conspiracy.

Hailed by Katherine Stone as "emotional, compelling, and triumphant!", **PRIVATE SCANDALS** is the debut novel by very talented Christy Cohen. From the glamour of New York to the glitter of Hollywood comes a heartfelt story of scandalous desires and long-held secrets . . . of dreams realized and longings denied . . . of three remarkable women whose lifelong friendship would be threatened by one man.

Available once again is **A LOVE FOR ALL TIME** by bestselling author Dorothy Garlock. In this moving tale, Casey Farrow gives up all hope of a normal life when a car crash leaves indelible marks on her breathtaking beauty . . . until Dan Farrow, the man who rescued her from the burning vehicle, convinces her that he loves her just the way she is.

Also on sale this month in the hardcover edition from Doubleday is **THE LADY AND THE CHAMP** by Fran Baker. When a former Golden Gloves champion meets an elegant, uptown girl, the result is a stirring novel of courageous love that Julie Garwood has hailed as "unforgettable."

Happy reading!

With warmest wishes,

Nita Taublib

Nita Taublib
Associate Publisher
LOVESWEPT and FANFARE

THE TIGER PRINCE
by Iris Johansen
the nationally bestselling author of
THE GOLDEN BARBARIAN

From the shimmering cities of a faraway land to the heather-scented hills of the Scottish Highlands comes this passionate tale of adventure and dangerous desire by one of America's bestselling and beloved authors.

In a locked room of shadows and sandalwood, Jane Barnaby first met the wickedly disturbing man whose searing blue eyes and brazen smile seemed to read her deepest desires—a man who exuded the mystery and danger of exotic lands. In his mesmerizing presence, Jane found herself instantly transformed from a hardheaded businesswoman to the willing slave of a passion she knew she must resist.

In the following scene from the opening pages of the novel, we see how a young Jane Barnaby tries to escape the poverty of the American west to begin her world-spanning adventure. . . .

Promontory Point, Utah
November 25, 1869

"Wait!"

Dear God, he hadn't heard her. He was still striding across the wooden platform toward the train. In a moment he would be out of reach.

Panic soared through Jane Barnaby and she broke into a run, the faded skirts of her calico gown ballooning behind her. Ignoring the pain caused by the ice shards piercing her feet through the holes in the thin soles of her boots, she tore through ice-coated mud puddles down the wheel-rutted street toward the platform over a hundred yards away. "Please! Don't go!"

Patrick Reilly's expression was only a blur in the post-dawn grayness, but he must have heard her call, for he hesitated for an instant before continuing toward the train, his long legs quickly covering the distance between the station house and the passenger railway car.

He was leaving her.

Fear caught in her throat, and she desperately tried to put on more speed. The train was already vibrating, puffing, flexing its metal muscles as it prepared to spring forward down the track. "Wait for me!"

He kept his face turned straight ahead, ignoring her.

Anger, fired by desperation, flared within her and she bellowed, "Dammit, do you hear me? Don't you *dare* get on that train!"

He stopped in midstride, his big shoulders braced militantly beneath the gray-checked coarse wool of his coat. He turned with a frown to watch her dashing toward him down the platform.

She skidded to a stop before him. "I'm goin' with you."

"The hell you are. I told you last night at Frenchie's you were to stay here."

"You gotta take me."

"I don't have to do nothin'." He scowled down at her. "Go back to your ma. She'll be looking for you."

"No, she won't." She took a step closer to him. "You know all she cares about is her pipe. She don't care where I am. She won't mind if I go with you."

He shook his head.

"You know it's true." Jane moistened her lips. "I'm goin' with you. She doesn't want me. She never wanted me."

"Well, I don't want you to eith—" A flush deepened his already ruddy cheeks, and his Irish brogue thickened as he said awkwardly, "No offense, but I don't have no use for a kid in my life."

"I'm not so little, I'm almost twelve." It was only a small lie; she had just turned eleven, but he probably wouldn't remember that. She took another step closer. "You gotta take me. I belong to you."

"How many times do I have to tell you? I'm not your father."

"My mother said it was most likely you." She touched a strand of the curly red hair flopping about her thin face. "Our hair is the same, and you visited her a lot before she went on the pipe."

"So did half the men of the Union Pacific." His expression softened as he suddenly knelt in front of her. "Lots of Irishmen have red hair, Jane. Hell, I can name four men on my own crew who used to be Pearl's regulars. Why not pick on one of them?"

Because she desperately wanted it to be him. He was kinder to her than any of the other men who paid her mother for her body. Patrick Reilly was drunk more than he was sober when he came to Frenchie's tent, but he never hurt the women like some men did and even treated Jane with a rough affection whenever he saw her around. "It's you." Her jaw set stubbornly. "You can't know for certain it's not you."

His jaw set with equal obstinance. "And you don't know for certain it is me. So why don't you go back to Frenchie's and leave me alone? Christ, I wouldn't even know how to take care of you."

"Take care of me?" She stared at him in bewilderment. "Why should you do that? I take care of myself."

For an instant a flicker of compassion crossed his craggy

features. "I guess you've had to do enough of that all right. With your ma sucking on that damn opium pipe and growing up in that pimp's hovel."

She immediately pounced on the hint of softening. "I won't be a bother to you. I don't eat much and I'll stay out of your way." He was beginning to frown again, and she went on hurriedly. "Except when you have something for me to do, of course. I'm a hard worker. Ask anyone at Frenchie's. I empty slops and help in the kitchen. I sweep and mop and run errands. I can count and take care of money. Frenchie even has me time the customers on Saturday night and tell them when they've had their money's worth." She grasped his arm. "I promise I'll do anything you want me to do. Just take me with you."

"Hell, you don't under—" He was silent a moment, gazing at her pleading face before muttering, "Look, I'm a railroad man. It's all I know and my job here is over now that the tracks have been joined. I've got an offer to boss my own crew in Salisbury and that's a big chance for an ignorant mick like me. Salisbury's way across the ocean in England. You don't want to go that far away."

"Yes, I do. I don't care where we go." Her small hand tightened on his arm. "Try me. I promise you won't be sorry."

"The devil I won't be sorry." His tone was suddenly impatient as he shook off her grasp and rose to his feet. "I won't be saddled with no whore's kid for the rest of my life. Go back to Frenchie's." He started toward the train again.

The rejection frightened but didn't surprise her. She had been rejected all her life by everyone but the inhabitants of Frenchie's crib and had learned long ago she wasn't like the children of the respectable wives who followed the railroad crews from town to town. They belonged in a world of clean crisp gowns, Saturday night baths, and church on Sunday mornings while she . . .

Jane felt suddenly sick as memories flooded back to her of the lantern-lit haze of Frenchie's tent, where the cots were separated only by dirty blankets hung on sagging ropes, the sweetish smell of the opium her mother smoked from the funny-looking glass bowl by her cot, Frenchie's hard palm striking her cheek when she wasn't quick enough to do his bidding.

She *couldn't* go back to that now that escape was so near.

Her nails dug into her palms as her hands clenched into fists at her sides. "It will do you no good to leave me. I'll only follow you."

He reached the train and placed his left foot on the metal step.

"I *will*. You belong to me."

"The hell I do."

"I'll follow you to this Saddlebury and—"

"Salisbury, and you'd have to swim the goddamn ocean."

"I'll do it. I'll find a way. You'll see that I'll find a way to—" Her voice broke and she had to stop.

"Dammit." His head lowered, his gaze fixed on the ridged metal of the step. "Why the hell do you have to be so damned stubborn?"

"Take me," she whispered. She did not know what else to say, what to offer him. "Please. If I stay, I'm scared someday I'll be like her. I . . . don't like it there."

He stood there, his shoulders hunched as moment after moment passed. "Oh, what the hell!" He whirled, jumped back down on the platform. His big, freckled hands grasped her waist and he effortlessly picked her up and lifted her onto the train. "Jesus, you're tiny. You don't weigh anything at all."

Had he given in? She was afraid to believe it. "That doesn't matter. I'm small for my age, but I'm very strong."

"You'd better be. I guess you can trail along, but it don't mean anything. I'm not your father and you'll call me Patrick like anybody else."

LADY DEFIANT
by Suzanne Robinson

Author of LADY GALLANT and LADY HELLFIRE

"An author with star quality . . . spectacularly talented."
—*Romantic Times*

As the queen's most cunning spy, Blade Fitzstephen knew where his duty lay. Sent to romance Oriel Richmond into revealing a dangerous secret the lovely innocent did not even know she possessed, he was prepared to go to any lengths to captivate her. Oriel knew that her many lovelorn suitors were more taken with her fortune than with her beauty. Yet when she overheard the only man who had ever stirred her interest—the dark and roguish Blade—describe her in highly unflattering terms, she was more than hurt, she was furious. Never again would she harbor dreams of love . . . until the day Blade returned to Richmond Hall to press his suit, and Oriel found herself responding against all reason. . . .

If you loved LADY GALLANT, don't miss Blade's own sensuous, romantic story in LADY DEFIANT.

"May God damn you to the eternal fires," Blade said.

Oriel had been about to push the door open, but paused as she heard the young man speak. The father said nothing. His mouth was full and he chewed calmly.

"This is the fourth girl you've dragged me to see, and the worst. She's also the last."

"Clean her up and she'll be worth looking over. Jesu Maria, did you see that wild hair? Almost black, but with so much red to it there must be a spirit of fire in her to match."

"I care not. Did you think to buy my return to your side with a virgin sacrifice?"

"It's your duty to stay by my side and produce heirs."

"God's breath!" Blade took several steps toward his father, then halted and cursed again as he tried to strangle the hilt of his sword with one hand. "I won't do it. I won't marry her. She has eyes like dried peas and a pointy little face like a weasel, and she can't even remember my name."

"It's Blade." Oriel pushed the door back and stepped into the great chamber.

It had taken all her courage not to run away. His disdain had been so unexpected. He'd said those words so quickly she hadn't understood their meaning immediately, and then she realized that while she had been enraptured, he had been offended by her and her appearance. All the years of encountering youths and men who paid her slight notice came thundering back into her memory. The evenings spent watching while others danced, the hunts spent pursuing a deer or fowl while other girls were instead pursued themselves—these had driven her to seek comfort in learning and solitary pursuits.

Until today she'd scorned to seek the favor of men, for there lay the path to great hurt. She had forgotten herself and her fear this once, for the prize entranced her without warning, danced before her in the guise of a dark-haired lord with eyes like the silver edge of a cloud when lit by the sun behind it. She had forgotten, and now she paid the price.

When she'd spoken, both men had frozen. Neither had spoken as she entered, and now Blade approached her. Oriel held up a hand to stop him, and he hesitated.

"If it please you, my lord, let there be no pretense between us." Oriel stopped and swallowed, for her voice trembled. "I see that you like not my person and have no time or desire to make yourself familiar with my character. Likewise, I find myself unable to countenance a suitor with so ungentle a manner, be he ever so handsome and endowed with a goodly estate."

"Mistress, my hot and heady language was the result of being near my lord father."

"Whatever the cause, I have no wish to deal with you further. Good day to you, my lords."

Oriel turned her back on Blade and made herself walk slowly out of the great chamber, down the gallery to the staircase. She lifted her skirts and was about to dash upstairs in a race to beat the fall of her tears when she heard Blade's voice calling to her.

He was at her side before she could retreat. His cloak swirled around her skirts, and his dark form blocked out the light from the gallery windows. She could smell the leather of his riding clothes. He put a hand on her arm, and she sprang away, shaking it off.

"Mistress, stay you a moment."

"I have work, my lord." She must gain her chamber before she betrayed herself with tears.

"I swear to you, my words were hastily spoken and ill-reasoned on account of my anger at my father. A meanness of spirit overcomes me when I'm in his company for long, and this time I struck out at him and hit you instead. I take an oath before God that none of my insults are true."

"Ofttimes we speak our truest feelings when our words are least guarded, my lord."

She brushed past him and mounted the stairs with as much dignity as she could summon. Halfway up he was still looking at her from below.

"Lady, I go to France soon, and would not leave this kingdom without your forgiveness."

Oriel looked down at Blade. Even from this height he appeared as tall as a crusader tower and as beautiful as a thunderstorm in July. In a brief span she had been enthralled and rejected, and if she didn't get away from him she would throw herself on the floor and weep for what she had lost almost before she knew she wanted it.

"Of course. As a good Christian I can hardly withhold my forgiveness, and you have it. It seems to be the only thing in Richmond Hall you want. Once again, good day to you, my lord."

PRIVATE SCANDALS
by Christy Cohen

From the glamour of New York to the glitter of Hollywood, PRIVATE SCANDALS is a heartfelt story of scandalous desires and long-held secrets . . . of dreams realized and longings denied . . . of three remarkable women whose lifelong friendship would be threatened by one man.

She stood rigid as steel, her eyes cast downward, and Jackson felt a familiar sickly dread gnaw at his gut. She must have changed her mind, and this time there would be no second chances for him.

When the minister asked her to repeat her vows, she raised her head. Her gaze met his, and a warm flood of relief washed over Jackson. Her eyes, so clear and beautiful, were sure and strong and loving. She spoke her promises firmly, confidently, with the smooth voice he'd come to love as he loved no other. And when they sealed their marriage with a kiss, her lips were soft and trusting, and he could sense the smile that tugged at their corners.

In the receiving line she stood beside him, his wife, with the satin sleeve of her dress brushing against his arm. Her expression was bright and happy as she greeted their guests. He put his arm around her waist and marveled again at the way her body conformed to his so perfectly, filling in every crevice.

The guests filtered past, a blur of puckered lips and embracing arms. Jackson paid little attention. How could he when he had the woman of his dreams beside him? She brought him so much happiness, blanketed every aspect of his life with the gauze of perfection, that he often found the past forgotten, left behind like a child's blanket no longer needed for comfort. This woman gave him everything.

He was thinking of that, of the laughter that grew more frequent between them every day, of the house in New Hampshire that awaited them, when he felt her squeeze his hand. Turning quickly, he saw the color drain from her face. He followed her desperate gaze and held himself steady against a wave of dizziness when he saw what she was looking at.

"She's here," his wife said needlessly, her silky voice marred by an uncharacteristic tremor. "I can't believe she's here."

He pulled her close to him and pressed his lips to her ear. "I love you."

She stood motionless for a moment, then he watched her transform. She pulled her scared, hunched body up straight again and smiled the smile that haunted men the world over. Her eyes met his, and he saw the tears filling them.

"And I you," she said, running her fingers along his cheek.

He returned his attention to the guests and watched, out of the corner of his eye, as she approached. He couldn't help being surprised by her beauty. It had been more than three years since he'd seen her, and she seemed to have grown softer, more feminine, more fragile. She was next in line to greet them, and the guilty pangs, long banished to the unnoticed, unwanted recesses of his mind, returned with violent intensity.

Finally, she stood before them, her chin up, her fists clenched. The woman he'd left behind. The woman once cherished as his wife's best friend. The woman who had loved him so much he couldn't breathe. She stood before them after years of bitter silence and, following a deep, drawn-out sigh, began to speak.

A LOVE FOR ALL TIME
by Dorothy Garlock

"[Dorothy Garlock] gets to the real heart and soul
of her characters."
—*Romantic Times*

**From award-winning author Dorothy Garlock
comes one of her most beloved classic romances—
a beautiful, moving story of love and beauty.**

*When she'd first woken up in the hospital, frightened and in pain,
only the gentle, masculine voice of a stranger had the power to soothe
Casey Farrow. Dan Murdock had dragged her from the wreckage of
her car and saved her life. He'd held her hand and lent her his
strength. But now, as she contemplated a future forever altered by the
scars that marred her body and ended her career, Casey wondered
why Dan was still there. . . .*

*She didn't want his pity. She didn't need his help. And when he told
her that he loved her, Casey thought he'd lost his mind. One look in
the mirror was enough to convince her that no man as attractive as
Dan Murdock could possibly want her . . . until the night he
showed her how wrong she could be. But wanting and loving are two
very different things, and now Casey wonders if theirs is truly a love
that can last for all time. . . .*

*Don't miss this classic Dorothy Garlock romance, available for the
first time in many years.*

OFFICIAL RULES TO WINNERS CLASSIC SWEEPSTAKES

No Purchase necessary. To enter the sweepstakes follow instructions found elsewhere in this offer. You can also enter the sweepstakes by hand printing your name, address, city, state and zip code on a 3" x 5" piece of paper and mailing it to: Winners Classic Sweepstakes, P.O. Box 785, Gibbstown, NJ 08027. Mail each entry separately. Sweepstakes begins 12/1/91. Entries must be received by 6/1/93. Some presentations of this sweepstakes may feature a deadline for the Early Bird prize. If the offer you receive does, then to be eligible for the Early Bird prize your entry must be received according to the Early Bird date specified. Not responsible for lost, late, damaged, misdirected, illegible or postage due mail. Mechanically reproduced entries are not eligible. All entries become property of the sponsor and will not be returned.

Prize Selection/Validations: Winners will be selected in random drawings on or about 7/30/93, by VENTURA ASSOCIATES, INC., an independent judging organization whose decisions are final. Odds of winning are determined by total number of entries received. Circulation of this sweepstakes is estimated not to exceed 200 million. Entrants need not be present to win. All prizes are guaranteed to be awarded and delivered to winners. Winners will be notified by mail and may be required to complete an affidavit of eligibility and release of liability which must be returned within 14 days of date of notification or alternate winners will be selected. Any guest of a trip winner will also be required to execute a release of liability. Any prize notification letter or any prize returned to a participating sponsor, Bantam Doubleday Dell Publishing Group, Inc., its participating divisions or subsidiaries, or VENTURA ASSOCIATES, INC. as undeliverable will be awarded to an alternate winner. Prizes are not transferable. No multiple prize winners except as may be necessary due to unavailability, in which case a prize of equal or greater value will be awarded. Prizes will be awarded approximately 90 days after the drawing. All taxes, automobile license and registration fees, if applicable, are the sole responsibility of the winners. Entry constitutes permission (except where prohibited) to use winners' names and likenesses for publicity purposes without further or other compensation.

Participation: This sweepstakes is open to residents of the United States and Canada, except for the province of Quebec. This sweepstakes is sponsored by Bantam Doubleday Dell Publishing Group, Inc. (BDD), 666 Fifth Avenue, New York, NY 10103. Versions of this sweepstakes with different graphics will be offered in conjunction with various solicitations or promotions by different subsidiaries and divisions of BDD. Employees and their families of BDD, its division, subsidiaries, advertising agencies, and VENTURA ASSOCIATES, INC., are not eligible.

Canadian residents, in order to win, must first correctly answer a time limited arithmetical skill testing question. Void in Quebec and wherever prohibited or restricted by law. Subject to all federal, state, local and provincial laws and regulations.

Prizes: The following values for prizes are determined by the manufacturers' suggested retail prices or by what these items are currently known to be selling for at the time this offer was published. Approximate retail values include handling and delivery of prizes. Estimated maximum retail value of prizes: 1 Grand Prize ($27,500 if merchandise or $25,000 Cash); 1 First Prize ($3,000); 5 Second Prizes ($400 each); 35 Third Prizes ($100 each); 1,000 Fourth Prizes ($9.00 each) ; 1 Early Bird Prize ($5,000); Total approximate maximum retail value is $50,000. Winners will have the option of selecting any prize offered at level won. Automobile winner must have a valid driver's license at the time the car is awarded. Trips are subject to space and departure availability. Certain black-out dates may apply. Travel must be completed within one year from the time the prize is awarded. Minors must be accompanied by an adult. Prizes won by minors will be awarded in the name of parent or legal guardian.

For a list of Major Prize Winners (available after 7/30/93): send a self-addressed, stamped envelope entirely separate from your entry to: Winners Classic Sweepstakes Winners, P.O. Box 825, Gibbstown, NJ 08027. Requests must be received by 6/1/93. DO NOT SEND ANY OTHER CORRESPONDENCE TO THIS P.O. BOX.

FANFARE

The Very Best in Historical Women's Fiction

Rosanne Bittner

_____	28599-8	EMBERS OF THE HEART $4.50/5.50 in Canada
_____	28319-7	MONTANA WOMAN $4.99/5.99
_____	29033-9	IN THE SHADOW OF THE MOUNTAINS $5.50/6.99
_____	29014-2	SONG OF THE WOLF $4.99/5.99
_____	29015-0	THUNDER ON THE PLAINS $5.99/6.99

Kay Hooper

_____	29256-0	THE MATCHMAKER $4.50/5.50

Iris Johansen

_____	28855-5	THE WIND DANCER $4.95/5.95
_____	29032-0	STORM WINDS $4.99/5.99
_____	29244-7	REAP THE WIND $4.99/5.99
_____	29604-3	THE GOLDEN BARBARIAN $4.99/5.99

Teresa Medeiros

_____	29047-5	HEATHER AND VELVET $4.99/5.99

Patricia Potter

_____	29070-3	LIGHTNING $4.99/ 5.99
_____	29071-1	LAWLESS $4.99/ 5.99
_____	29069-X	RAINBOW $4.99/ 5.99

Fayrene Preston

_____	29332-X	THE SWANSEA DESTINY $4.50/5.50

Amanda Quick

_____	29325-7	RENDEZVOUS $4.99/5.99
_____	28354-5	SEDUCTION $4.99/5.99
_____	28932-2	SCANDAL $4.95/5.95
_____	28594-7	SURRENDER $4.50/5.50

Deborah Smith

_____	28759-1	THE BELOVED WOMAN $4.50/ 5.50

Ask for these titles at your bookstore or use this page to order.

Please send me the books I have checked above. I am enclosing $ _____ (add $2.50 to cover postage and handling). Send check or money order, no cash or C. O. D.'s please.

Mr./ Ms. _____

Address _____

City/ State/ Zip _____

Send order to: Bantam Books, Dept. FN 17, 2451 S. Wolf Road, Des Plaines, IL 60018

Please allow four to six weeks for delivery.

Prices and availability subject to change without notice.

FN 17 - 8/92